The October People

Book One

A Gulf Coast Paranormal Extra

By M.L. Bullock

Dedication

For Juno

Prologue—Hugh McCandlish

Leaf Academy, Orange Grove, Alabama, 1937

"Good job, Ollie. Why don't you leave the drawing on my desk? What an artist you have become, young man."

As he placed the picture on my desk, my heart fell to see the subject of his most recent drawing. Did he blame himself for the incident on the playground? He should not blame himself for the bird's death. He never touched the creature. Perhaps this was some sort of tribute to it? Or more probably I was reading too much into the drawing. Perhaps this austere-looking bird was a raven? We recently discussed the poetic works of Edgar Allan Poe, and the American crow and the common raven were very similar. Ravens were notably larger and traveled in pairs; crows were almost always in large groups. It was hard to tell from this image. It was only a single bird, its head perched at an awkward angle, yet the imagery evoked such intense, brooding emotion.

I smiled as I set the paper aside and asked, "I suppose you will be happy to see your father again, Ollie. Are both your parents coming to pick you up tomorrow? I hope to meet them. Are you looking forward to a visit home?"

The boy's long bangs fell over his dark, distrusting eyes. He shook his head, returned his pencils to his desk and left the classroom. He paused at the door as if he wanted to tell me something, but he did not. He did not talk much at all. His mouth was set in a perpetual frown these days, such a far cry from the high-spirited child who had arrived here last month. But the truth was that transitioning to life at boarding school was not easy for some children, even those from good families. It was always easier if you had a friend—I knew that from experience—but this child had none. I could not understand that.

Ollie LeFlore had a constantly solemn appearance, a characteristic that the other boys disliked. They made no secret of it, but they didn't bully him or abuse him, not in front of me. They simply ignored him. I encouraged Ollie to interact with the others, but he never made the effort. And the recent Dead Crow Incident would not help matters. I suppose it wasn't strange after all that he should want to draw the creature in such perfect detail.

The bird had been cawing and crowing as it perched on the metal fence that surrounded the athletic yard. A few of the boys had taken to throwing rocks at it but were cuffed about the ears by the headmaster for their trouble. When we turned our attention back to the animal, it was lying dead at Ollie's feet. The other boys were backing away as if he might kill them too. Nobody saw anything, and as I explained to the headmaster, if Ollie had killed the bird, the boy would have been covered with scratches, claw marks...but there was nothing to see, and I had examined the boy myself. It was as if the bird died of natural causes, falling out of the sky right at the child's feet.

But the odds of that happening were astronomical.

The night of the strange event, I began to work out the numbers. Coming up with the proper formula proved a challenge, and the results were indeed astronomical. One would have a better chance of being struck by lightning—twice—than having a bird fall out of the sky and land at one's feet. But what other explanation could there be? Yes, the bird must have been sickly. It had been Ollie's misfortune that it died that day, at that moment.

Yes, such a rare occurrence.

Mrs. Smith, the school's cook, had her own ideas about the dead crow. And she had no problem sharing those ideas with anyone who would listen...except for the headmaster, of course. "This place, this school is cursed, Mr. McCandlish. It was cursed long before they built this fine building here. The very grounds we walk on are cursed."

I laughed a little and took a green apple from the wooden bowl on the counter. "Yet you work here, dear. What makes you say such a thing, Mrs. Smith?"

"Work here, yes. Live here, no. Never. You couldn't pay me enough copper for that. Everyone knows about the October People. This was their land before it went to the Leaf Academy."

I laughed again, trying to cheer her and myself. Why the mention of the October People should chill me to the bone, I did not understand. Perhaps she was just upset that the school was closed for the fall holiday? I could not think of a reason she would speak so darkly about a local legend.

"The October People? That sounds like a fantastic tale. And what is the difference? If the place were cursed, it would matter little whether you worked here, lived here or only visited. I never knew that curses were so discerning, Mrs. Smith. I think you are having me on; a bit of laughter at the foreigner's expense? I'll have ye know that my own Nanna was a far better storyteller than you, madam. Besides, if you really believed this place cursed, you would na darken the doorway, would you?"

"There *is* a difference, and I would think you would know it. But it being your first semester here, maybe you don't. Tell me, Mr. McCandlish, before you laugh me off, you don't think it is strange, them shutting down the school for the entire month of October? It happens every year, and I can tell you why. We all know why. We leave for the month so The Others can come." She crossed herself before continuing her peeling and cutting of the apples. Her helper, a young lady named Emma, did the same and scurried out with food scraps to take to the pigs. Apparently, Emma did not want to be a part of this conversation. Not in the least.

"Ah yes, the October People."

"Mock me if you like. We all know about the crow, we down here in the kitchen. It is a sign. Mark my words—they are coming. Birds don't just fall out of the sky, sir. No, they don't. Be careful, Mr. McCandlish. Be very careful indeed."

Mrs. Smith was always going on about spooks and haints of one sort or another, but I never put much stock in such ideas. There was nothing she could tell me that would be more frightening than my own grandmother's knotted tales about the McCandlish ghosts that wandered the broken stones of the ancestral castle. I had never seen those venerated stones or any ghosts, and I took my Nanna's and Mrs. Smith's words for what they were, a way of keeping naughty boys in line. But I was no naughty child. I was a grown man and a long way from Scotland.

As nonchalantly as possible, I took a bite of the apple. "Come now, Mrs. Smith. I hope you do not repeat these things to the children. I daresay you may frighten a few of them."

"Not all of them," she said as she waved her shiny knife at the shadow in the doorway. It was Ollie LeFlore. He must have followed me to the kitchen, or he came seeking a treat. I sincerely hoped he had heard none of this conversation. I stole another apple from the bowl and ignored Mrs. Smith's disapproving glance.

"All packed, Ollie?" I handed him the apple as we stepped out into the chilly corridor and left the warm kitchen behind. It was the last day of September, too early in the year for truly cold weather, but I could feel the fingers of fall reaching toward us. I recognized autumn's approach, and the chilliness threatened to permeate my old bones. Unlike the headmaster, Mr. Mitchell, I did not mind the heat of the North American South at all. After nearly a lifetime in chilly northern Scotland, the warm temperatures of Alabama were a boon to my body and my soul. It was always easier to get up in the morning here.

"What's on your mind, then? Out with it. I'll have none of yer sulking."

"No one is coming for me."

I paused mid-bite and squatted down in front of the small boy with the dark eyes and quivering lips. I could see he had been crying, which was very unusual for him. Very unusual indeed. "What do you mean? You mean none of your family are coming today? Ach, na, lad. Surely they will be here tomorrow. They have only been delayed."

"No." He clutched the apple, and a shadow passed over his face. I turned to see the headmaster standing behind me.

"There you are, Mr. McCandlish. I had hoped to find you before I left. We have a bit of a problem, sir. If you will come with me."

I glanced at Ollie, whose expression never changed. I offered him my hand, but he did not take it. The three of us walked into the headmaster's office, and I took a seat on the bench across his desk as he closed the door. Ollie lingered at my shoulder as if I were his protector. Had he been up to something naughty?

"Troubling news, Mr. McCandlish. I hear you plan to stay here at the Leaf Academy instead of taking your holiday off campus. Surely you remember that this is against the rules. There is to be no one here for the month of October." I tossed the apple in the nearby trash can. It made an unusually heavy, dull thump as it landed, like a cannonball dropping to the ground. "This puts me in a very bad position, I am afraid. We have a very strict rule here—everyone, without exception, leaves for the fall holiday, Mr. McCandlish. It is tradition, and more than that, it is a requirement. It says so in your contract."

I glanced over at Ollie standing by the door. It made me sick to see Mr. Mitchell ignore him so, but that was his way. Mr. Mitchell was headmaster, true enough, but he never interacted with the children except to administer discipline or distribute awards at our quarterly events. "But surely the academy can make an exception this time. Ollie has just told me— no, don't sulk, lad. He has just told me that no one is coming to pick him up. He is quite alone, sir." I swallowed at my excuse. Of course, I'd had no such excuse before a few minutes ago and I had planned to stay here at the Leaf Academy before I knew Ollie was in need, but that was beside the point now.

Mr. Mitchell stroked his slightly over-greased mustache as he thought about my plea. "You say a boy is in need?" The headmaster paled but still did not acknowledge Ollie at all.

"Yes, come, Ollie. Come tell the headmaster what you told me." The boy walked over, his hands by his sides, his head down. "Speak up now. Don't be shy, lad."

"No one is coming for me," Ollie said without looking up. His dark hair hung in his eyes. I would have to see that he got a haircut and soon. The headmaster would certainly complain about the length. *No fops here, boys. No fops at the Leaf Academy.*

Mr. Mitchell shot up like an arrow being released from a bow. He moved so quickly that I jumped up too. What was going on here?

The headmaster was visibly shaken at the news but offered no solace to young LeFlore. "There will be no staff here, Mr. McCandlish. No one to cook, clean or tend to your needs. Or anyone else's, for that matter. I daresay there is room at the Yellow Rose Hotel; that is the closest place. It would be better for you to stay there." Ollie began to cry, and the apple fell from his hand and hit the ground with a plunk. Mitchell's knuckles whitened as he moved behind his chair and clutched the leather back.

"There now, lad. We will figure this out. I am sorry about your family, Ollie. Putting the boy up in a hotel seems a bit risky. He is only a child, Mr. Mitchell. Surely he could spend his holiday with one of us. We could write to his father and ask his permission."

"There is no time for that. Tomorrow is the first of October. Nobody stays here in October. In fact, the staff is leaving tonight after supper. If you stay here, McCandlish, I want you to understand that you will be alone. Quite alone for the entire month."

I was a grown man and could tend to myself, and I welcomed the silence. I had books to read, and there was an interesting star alignment predicted for the middle of the month. I had spent a month's pay on the proper telescope and equipment. I planned to map and record the entire three-day event. But this unexpected turn of events threatened to force my hand. Should I confess to the headmaster what I had planned? No, he did not seem to care now.

"I assure you I will be fine, Mr. Mitchell. I cannot in good conscience leave the Leaf Academy with Ollie's future so uncertain. I will remain until someone comes for him. Surely, you can understand the need here."

"On your own head be it then, Mr. McCandlish." He grimaced as he leaned forward, his pen in hand. "As headmaster of the Leaf Academy, I grudgingly give you permission to remain for the holiday. You are a good man, McCandlish, perhaps too good."

"Thank you, Headmaster. I shall do my best to keep Ollie occupied until his parents arrive."

"And then you will leave. No lingering about, McCandlish."

"I will absolutely not linger about, Mr. Mitchell," I lied quite easily. "Thank you, sir. Come, Ollie."

We left the headmaster behind and walked down the narrow hall that led to the two staircases, one to the teachers' wing and the other to the students' dormitory. The place was already as quiet as a church. There was no laughter, no shuffling of books or scraping of chairs. Hardly any noise at all.

"Ollie, bring your things to my room. You know where it is, don't you? It's the last door on the left, down the hall there. You can bunk with me. We will be like two friends spending the holiday together."

"We aren't leaving? What will we do when The Others come? They won't like that we are here."

I smiled up at the boy as I squatted down in front of him and he rubbed his red nose with his coat sleeve. "What do you know about the October People? Have you been listening to Mrs. Smith and her stories? It's all rubbish, lad. I don't know exactly what our plans will be, but we will be together. I promise you that. I won't leave you. I will just have to keep you entertained until your parents can retrieve you."

In a surprising gesture, Ollie put his arms around my neck. He hugged me but then released me quickly, running down the hall to fetch his undoubtedly meager things. I felt a shiver at my shoulder. I glanced behind me, but there was no one. Not even a shadow on the wall.

Jumping at shadows now, are we? Too many of Mrs. Smith's stories, McCandlish.

No, it wasn't that. It was something the boy said that gave me the goose-willies.

They won't like that we are here...

Humming quietly to myself, I walked to my room and began rearranging furniture. Surely there was enough room to drag a cot into my quarters. We would make it comfortable and cozy. It would be perfect. I wouldn't be lonely, and Ollie was quiet enough. He might enjoy studying the stars too.

What will we do when The Others come?

And what would Mrs. Smith say when she discovered we stayed the entire month and there were no Others? No October People. No curse. I smiled at that idea. I was one to enjoy disproving such things. *See, Nanna? It was only the wind blowing the curtains. No high spirits here.* And I had been looking for a new subject to study. Why not something like this? I could imagine the headlines now.

Local Teacher Puts Local Legend to Rest

Or better still...

Tenured Professor Debunks Local Legend

Surely they would offer me tenure for such an achievement. Yes, that's exactly what I would do. Ollie and I together. And when it was over, we would have a good laugh together, the lad and I.

A shadow crossed my door. I thought perhaps it was the headmaster or Ollie returned with his suitcase, but there was no one there. No one at all. I stepped out into the hallway and glanced around. No, there was nothing to see.

Just a black feather. Surprised to find it, I picked it up and laid it on my desk. *Better still, I should hide it. No reason to upset the boy.* I opened a drawer and squirreled it away for closer inspection later.

As I closed the drawer, Ollie stepped into the room, a looming shadow behind him. But when I blinked, the shadow vanished and only the smiling boy remained.

"Come inside, Ollie. Close the door. All is well now."

The door closed with a creak.

Chapter One—Jocelyn Graves

Mobile, Alabama, Today

"You know how much I enjoy working with you—the whole Gulf Coast Paranormal team—but I can't commit to another team investigation right now. That last investigation was one I will never forget, but I've got something I have to take care of first, Midas." I pretended I didn't notice his sigh of exasperation echoing through the phone.

Don't feel bad, my friend. I have that effect on people. Just ask anyone who knows me.

Aaron, Gulf Coast Paranormal's newest team member and all-around sexy dude, knew all about how frustrating I could be, and it wasn't that I was playing hard to get. I *liked* Aaron, but I wasn't one to be ruled by my heart—or my hormones. If Aaron really wanted to know more about me, he could just ask Pete. If Pete wasn't still running from the Dogman. I couldn't believe he'd left us in the middle of an investigation, but there was no denying it. If I hadn't seen it with my own eyes, I might not have believed it. Yep, he took the van and left us high and dry. Granted, he came back a few minutes later—I mean, apparently even Peter Broadus had a conscience—but the fact was he'd left us. If I ever had doubts about whether breaking up with him had been the right thing to do, I didn't anymore. Totally the right thing. But I never second-guessed myself, not concerning matters of the heart. There was too much to see, too much to do in this great big world to settle down with someone who was anything less than amazing.

Pete was many things, but he'd never been amazing. He was more like a cluster.

Why was I thinking about him right now?

"You going solo again?"

I was sure Midas didn't mean to sound like my non-existent father, but he kinda did.

"It won't be the first time. I think I'll do just fine."

I'd just spent a solid week with the entire Gulf Coast Paranormal team, and yes, there were some advantages to having a team on an investigation, but solo gigs had perks too. Less equipment, less drama. I needed some "me" time, and the page that I was holding in my hand was my ticket to that adventure. I read the email again as Midas continued his pitch. The team was short one man since he "fired" Pete. I worked well with the team, everyone liked me. They were heading to Gulfport soon to investigate some abandoned fairgrounds. As much as I liked Midas, he wasn't changing my mind. I was ready to end the phone call so I could get packed and get on the road. Midas was my friend, but my adventure came with an expiration date.

"I promise you that I will think about it. I have to do this other thing first."

He paused for a moment. I knew Midas well enough to know that he was "reading" me, a skill he used when he wanted to protect you from something or just be nosy. That was Midas. He was everyone's Protector. On one hand, I appreciated that about him, but on the other...not so much. "Stop worrying," I said, frowning at myself in the mirror next to me. I put the paper down on the desk and sat in the wonky desk chair. My temporary apartment was a craphole, but at least it wasn't a hotel. Man, I looked a fright. My dreads needed twisting, my eyebrows needed plucking, and I was pale. I typically kept a year-round tan because of all the time I spent outdoors with my photography gig, but my color was fading fast. "I know how you feel about my investigating alone, but it is what it is. I'm not dead yet."

"That's a great motto. Maybe that should be your next tattoo."

I smiled at his sarcasm. "Maybe. I actually like that. I've been meaning to add to my collection."

"Have you forgotten the Sapphire Caves?" he asked me in an attempt at adding some humor to our conversation.

"No, and I haven't forgotten Crenshaw Road either. Dangerous situations happen, Midas, whether there are seven of us or just one or two. It's the nature of the beast."

"For Crenshaw Road, that's a good description for it. Are you sure I can't talk you into bringing someone along? If not me, then Cassidy or Aaron?"

I smiled and shook my head. "Midas Demopolis, stop being an old lady. I'm going by myself. This is a once-in-a-lifetime opportunity. It's only a two-day investigation. I think I can handle it. I'll call you when I'm done."

"At least tell me where you are going. Just to be on the safe side."

I thought about it but decided against it. Although I was certain he didn't mean it this way, telling him would mean I was officially a member of Gulf Coast Paranormal...and I still wasn't sure I wanted to stay in one spot. I mean, I liked this part of the Gulf Coast, I liked the team, but I also liked my freedom.

"Nu-uh. But I will call you when I get done, and I swear I'll have an answer for you."

"Fine, but be safe, Jocelyn. Don't take unnecessary risks. Getting the shot isn't worth breaking your leg. Or your head."

"Got it. No risks and no breakage. I have to go, Midas. Have a good one."

"Bye." He hung up, and I breathed a sigh of relief. I read the email again, aloud this time just to be sure I was reading it correctly.

My client, Mr. Holloway, grants you permission to photograph the property at 1100 Orange Pekoe Avenue for a period of no more than two days. When you've completed your photo shoot, please leave the key in the metal lockbox on the front porch. I will retrieve it later. Also, Mr. Holloway expects that you will send him copies of your photographs for his own study. Please contact us prior to submitting your work to any publications, including local newspapers, books, etc. Good luck.

Sincerely,

Adrian Shanahan

I held the key in my hand. It wasn't one of those cheap keys you could go have made at any big blue store. It was the old-fashioned kind with an interesting handle and was larger than any key I had.

I removed my leather necklace, slid the key on it and tied it around my neck. I couldn't lose it now. I sometimes had a habit of leaving things behind when I started investigating. Like my film case or an audio recorder. Man, this was exciting. The notorious Leaf Academy! Score!

I heard Sherman's toenails clicking on the floor beside me. *Dang it. I forgot all about my dog.* But was he really my dog? The poor guy had turned up on my porch not long after I moved into the apartment complex. I knocked on all the neighbors' doors and inquired with the management, but nobody recognized or claimed the animal. Nobody wanted the hairy, white furball with the soft black eyes and equally black nose. Seemed a shame. He had no collar and no tag, but he had obviously been someone's dog. He was house-trained and sweet, and he didn't bark much. I never planned to keep him, especially since my future was always so uncertain, but he was growing on me and there weren't any other options. I posted his picture on social media but hadn't gotten any responses yet. The local animal shelter informed me that they weren't a no-kill facility. If I left the dog there and he couldn't find a home in a week, he would be put down. I couldn't believe it. I couldn't stomach it. So he got a name, a collar and a place on the couch until I could figure it all out.

"Well, Sherm. I hate to do this, but I have to go away for a few days." I petted his head and rubbed his ears. He rewarded me with lots of licks. "I can't believe nobody has claimed you yet, Sherman. You are an awesome dog. You deserve a happy home. Sorry about the name, but I have never named a dog before."

He whined once and laid his chin on my thigh. *Shoot. It's like he knows I'm leaving.*

I snuggled with him for a few minutes and then went back to packing my equipment. I wasn't taking everything, just a few cameras and a bunch of audio recorders. I couldn't believe I was being given access to the Leaf Academy. The place had been closed since

1978. They couldn't keep it open after the location had been linked to multiple murders. Total creep-fest, or so I heard.

But what about Sherman?

After a few phone calls, I found a well-recommended kennel that had an opening. "It's only for a few days," I said to him as we pulled into the Happy Paws Boarding Kennel later that afternoon. "And there will be lots of other dogs to play with. You be a good boy, and I'll be back in just a few days. Okay?"

Another whine. With a sigh, I leashed him up and walked him into the kennel. I tried not to look him in the eye. I surveyed the place and mentally gave it a thumbs-up. The people appeared knowledgeable and attentive. I got the impression that they really cared about their guests. Sherman would be in good hands.

Despite all this, I drove away feeling as if I would never see him again. And I was going to miss him.

Don't be so dramatic, Jocelyn. How can you miss a dog you barely know? It's not like he is your childhood pet. You're letting Midas put the chilly bumps on you. You'll be back, and the dog will be fine.

I chose to believe the voice of grown-up Jocelyn and drove away without looking once in the rearview mirror. But for the first time in a long time, I regret-ted leaving someone behind.

And the tears were real.

Chapter Two—Jocelyn

I could see the place on my phone app, but the directions were leading me in circles. Take Orange Pekoe to Newt Circle. But where was Newt Circle? I couldn't keep driving around. It would be dark in a few hours, and I had cameras and other equipment to set up if I actually found the place. Thankfully, I had a paper map in the glove box for backup. I pulled over to the side of the road and spread the map on the hood. There was no one out here, which seemed kind of strange. Just a few streets over was a residential area with small houses practically built on top of one another. Yes, I could see Kennedy Street and recognized those buildings.

Oh wow. Now I see it.

The Leaf Academy, or the ruins that were once the prominent boys' school, was hidden behind dozens of old trees, mostly oaks with a few pines growing tall and wild. How had I missed this driveway and that building? *It's almost like the place wants to stay hidden, huh?* I hurried back to my car and grabbed my camera from the front seat. I scanned the area to make sure no one was around, since I sure didn't want to get robbed out here in the middle of nowhere, but there wasn't a soul. I locked the car and headed up the narrow driveway. My Nissan could probably manage to navigate it, but I wanted to walk the rest of the way, at least for a first viewing.

I flipped the camera on and removed the lens cap. There wasn't much to see from this distance, but I snapped a few photos anyway. My heart was racing, and I couldn't help but smile at the promise of a new adventure. The road wasn't in total disrepair. Someone had been using it, and recently. Hopefully not criminals. I could see tire tracks and fresh piles of red dirt that had been halfheartedly moved around with a rake. I wasn't quite so alone now. Birds were chirping, and squirrels dashed across the canopy of trees above me. Their playful skittering sent down showers of leaves. I snapped a picture of them but wasn't sure I got anything.

I was feeling anxious about my car. *Maybe I shouldn't have walked up here. I can't afford to lose my equipment—or my vehicle. Yeah, I should go back. If I can't see the school clearly here at this turn of the path, I'll do just that.*

But when I turned the corner and walked into the small clearing, looming in front of me was the abandoned Leaf Academy. A wave of sadness struck me. For sure, this was a sad place. That was my first impression. The front porch was supported by four columns; there were traces of faded paint on the bottom of the columns, but the tops were brown, like the rest of the building. There was an ornate doorway with tall windows beside it and three smaller ones above it. There appeared to be two wings to the academy, and all the windows looked quite firmly boarded up. I wondered what secrets that dark, dirty space held...whether it was haunted or not, it sure as heck looked like it could be.

Snap, snap.

I took a flurry of pictures. First impressions were important when investigating. This was my favorite part. For sure, I couldn't believe my luck. Jocelyn Graves, amateur photographer, freelance writer and part-time paranormal investigator, was about to spend two whole days here at the Leaf Academy. The only price I had to pay was sending copies of my photos to the owner and doing a small write-up about any experiences I had here. Yep, I was one lucky gal. I shifted the camera and held it to my face as I snapped a dozen more photographs. Not too high a price for access to such a time capsule. With any luck, there would be some great artifacts inside. Maybe some classroom equipment or personal items. Those made the best subjects for photos.

I stood in silence for a few minutes as I paced and then walked the front yard as best I could. There was much more to see, but it would have to wait. I had to bring the car up, but I hesitated. I waited for something. My watch beeped, reminding me that I didn't have all day to stand here gawking at this potential paranormal playground. There was work to be done before the actual work could be done, and I was burning daylight. I snapped a few more pictures of the upstairs windows, especially the one on the end there. I didn't *see* anything at all since they were all boarded up, but I could not shake the feeling that there *was* someone inside. Waiting for me.

But there wasn't. Man, I had one heck of an imagination.

It was a fine brick building. Great details too. I hoped tomorrow would be sunnier. I needed all the light I could get for better shots. It was dark back here with so many trees surrounding the place. With a sigh of satisfaction, I began my walk back to the car, looking behind me a few times. Nope. Still nothing in that window. I made the turn that led to the drive and quickly returned with my car. I drove up to the house without incident. It wasn't the smoothest ride, but I'd been down roads that were a lot worse. Recently too.

"Okay, Leaf Academy. It's you and me now," I said as I closed the trunk and walked toward the front door with the two largest cases in my hands. Best to get the heavy lifting done early. I glanced up at the amazing front door again.

The front door that now stood wide open.

And not just a crack. It was all the way open as if someone expected me and wanted me to make myself at home. As I set the camera cases down on the ground, my knees felt a tad bit wobbly. *This isn't right. No way is this right.*

Removing the camera from around my neck, I scanned back through the photos. There! The door was closed. Completely closed! I looked at all the pictures, and it was clearly shut in every one of them.

Okay, Jocelyn. Let's think logically.

If the door wasn't closed good, if the lock was rusty or broken...any of those could explain why the door stood open now. Granted, there should have been some wind or a breeze or something to move that door, but I didn't feel a thing. In fact, it was unseasonably muggy. *Let's take this step by step.*

I walked up the steps and remembered Midas' warning. No broken legs, not this time around. There were a few spongy spots in the flooring, but nothing gave way. With my camera ready, I took shots of the porch, the doorframe, the open door. A fluttering darkness shot past the door but didn't make a sound. Was that some kind of bird in there? No, I would have heard wings, right?

With shaking fingers, I touched the rusty doorknob. It felt cooler than the air around it. Much cooler. *But that's not evidence. Take a look at the lock, Jocelyn.* I examined the doorknob and turned it. It moved, but it hadn't been greased for a while; it was one of those crafty old mechanisms that needed a good oiling every now and then. Each turn came with a subtle squeak. I closed the door and untangled the leather string around my neck. I shoved the key in the door lock and turned the knob, confirming that the lock was working. The door wouldn't swing open by just bumping it. In fact, I had a difficult time reopening the thing with the key. But eventually, it worked. The door opened easily now. I closed it again, stepped back and took a few more pictures. Nice craftsmanship. I didn't know how I missed it before, but above the door were some words carved into a piece of fitted stone. Latin, from the looks of it.

Non timebo mala.

Why did that sound so familiar? I whispered the phrase a few times to help me commit it to memory. Then I walked back to pick up my cases, navigated the steps carefully and approached the door with the key in my hand.

And it was open again.

Okay, Jocelyn Graves. You can write this down. Day one, hour one, paranormal evidence. But at least they want you here. Then that phrase came back to me. I'd seen it before, in a tattoo shop in Fort Lauderdale. I'd almost gotten that one but opted for the wildflower on my ankle. I much preferred icons over phrases as far as tattoos went.

But I knew what this meant. *Non timebo mala.* I will fear no evil.

Chapter Three—Jocelyn

The downstairs was a complete dust bowl despite the fact that every window on the bottom floor was boarded up. Leaving my cases in the front room, I removed the LED flashlight from my pocket and flicked it on. It cast a light blue light around the spacious foyer. There wasn't much to see in here, a built-in bench with hooks for rain gear. But what was that? I could see a door that led to a small office. I poked my head inside but didn't see anything interesting in here either. Basic office furniture, a desk, a broken metal chair and some sagging built-in bookcases. No personal effects at all except a calendar from 1957 and a faded picture in a dirty frame. But I would definitely ransack that desk later.

I walked out of the room and closed the door behind me. Standard procedure when investigating old houses, asylums, hospitals—always close the door behind you. So, now what? I had a few choices, go left, go right or go upstairs. Common sense said clear the bottom floor, make sure there were no vagrants or vandals on the premises, but I wasn't listening to my common sense right this moment. My proverbial sixth sense was tingling. Immediately I began photographing the foyer and then climbed the steps carefully. If I had any hope of sneaking up on anyone, all that was shot. With every step I took in my hiking boots, a floorboard creaked beneath me.

Strange. The window over the landing wasn't boarded up. I was glad for the light, but the glass was so dirty it didn't illuminate much. It cast the stairs in a dingy pale sepia color. No, I think it cast more shadows on the second floor. And that's where I was now.

Non timebo mala. What a strange phrase for a school. I mean, as if going to boarding school wasn't terrifying enough, seeing that would put the fear of God in you. Or the fear of something.

There was no office on the second level, not like the lower level. Clearly this floor was strictly for housing. Right at the top of the stairs, there was an open area with a few worn chairs and some other junk. I had the choice to go left or right and went to the right. There were rooms on either side of the corridor; all the rooms facing the front yard were boarded up. The rooms at the back, however, the ones facing the woods, were not. That was weird. Why board up the front and not the back? More than one window on the back side was broken.

Snap, snap.

But this level felt like it had been abandoned more recently. Odd personal items littered the floor. I could see an old tennis shoe, a rusty toy truck, an old-fashioned chalk slate and a broken wooden toy. I photographed them all as I made my way down the corridor. *Yeah, it's like the folks on this level just left and forgot to take their stuff with them. That is odd.*

I came to my senses after a few minutes of photographing various finds and dug my digital recorder out of my pocket. I clicked the button and began to ask the standard questions. "I'm on the second floor of the Leaf Academy. I felt compelled to check these rooms out first. My name is Jocelyn; what is your name?"

I walked to the window and set the recorder on the windowsill as I took in the view. At least there were no broken windows in this room. But there was also not one stick of furniture and not much of a view. Nothing to see but woods. Gosh, the sun was going down quickly. Too quickly. I'd have to finish setting up, but I had already decided that this would be the room; this would be HQ for the next few days.

"I hope you don't mind, but I am going to hang around for a few days. I brought my own cot and a pillow. Would you mind if I stayed in here?"

I shivered at my own question. I didn't hear a word, but I was convinced that I would hear something once I reviewed the tape. Yeah, I was pretty confident about that. "I am going to take pictures too. Would you like to take a picture? May I take yours?" I snapped a few shots but still nothing. I wasn't alarmed. Not frightened, not apprehensive. Instead, I got the strange sensation that I was expected, that whoever was here wanted me here.

Now that is a worrying thought.

"Non timebo mala...do you know what that means?"

A clicking in the hallway caught me off guard. It was the exact same sound my camera made, only I wasn't taking pictures in the hallway. And there was no possible way that was an echo; that's not how acoustics worked. I took another shot of the empty corner and silently counted off seconds; when I got to ten, I heard it again.

What in the Sam Hill?

I walked into the hallway and looked around. I took another picture just for the heck of it. I counted off again and waited. Nothing. *Hmm...maybe I'm making too much of it.* I stepped back into the room and returned to the previous spot.

"Is that you taking pictures in the hall? Are you taking my picture? I think I hear you. Can you do it again?" I waited another minute, but the phantom photographer did not repeat the sound. "I tell you what. I will leave my camera here on the windowsill. You can use it if you like. See this button? If you touch it, it will make that sound. You can touch it, but don't break it. I will be right back."

I set the camera on the windowsill, pushing it back far enough so it wouldn't fall off, and checked my watch. It was now 4:45 p.m. and time to get this show on the road. If I came back and found photos on the camera after that time, I would know that I made contact with someone. Or something.

Boy, if that's the case, this would be record time, I think.

I hurried down the stairs, retrieved my cases and came back up. Nothing was moved, I heard nothing else, and I didn't bother with the camera or audio recorder yet. I had to make three more trips; by the third, I was winded. I set up my cot and removed my thermal camera and tripod. I was definitely putting these guys in this hallway. I set them up, then grabbed an extra digital camera and slipped off down the stairs to lock the door and check the bottom floor.

I didn't like it down here. How had the atmosphere changed that quickly? It wasn't cozy at all; in fact, it was kind of sickening. Kind of awful. The hallways were cluttered, and there were birds in some of the rooms as well as evidence of rodents. Yeah, I was glad I had decided to stay upstairs. It felt less decrepit on the second floor.

So, what's the plan, Jocelyn? What to do first?

From some of the reports, the auditorium, the big room to my right, was a hot spot for paranormal activity. I supposed the practical thing to do was spend some time in there. And then maybe take some shots in the backyard focusing on the windows. When I walked toward the auditorium, I turned just in time to see a feather falling to the ground.

And it appeared to have fallen out of thin air.

It was a big black feather, maybe from a raven or a crow. I ducked, expecting to see a bird circling me, but saw nothing. I heard birds, but they were tiny finches. Nothing as large as whatever this came from. I took a picture as it landed on the ground. Looking around the room again, I searched for the bird, but there was nothing to see.

Okay, reality check. No way did that float down from nowhere. You probably stirred up the feather when you walked past it, or it fell from a beam above you. There are all kinds of birds in this place. I took a few more pictures of the feather, and then I touched it briefly. It felt kind of crunchy, like it had been here a long while.

And then the hallway went completely silent. All the birds stopped chirping. Even the crickets outside got quiet, like they did whenever there was a predator nearby. When I camped with my grandparents growing up, that was our cue to hunker down. But I didn't see anything, and I sure wasn't a predator. Maybe there was something here I could not see?

That's when I decided it was time to move. The auditorium could wait for a little while. The investigator in me said, "Get in there!" Survivor-Jocelyn voted that down, at least for the time being. Time to go back upstairs and come up with a solid plan.

I put the feather back. I didn't want to touch it anymore.

It didn't belong to me.

Chapter Four—Hugh

The last of the staff left this morning, and I assured the groundskeeper that I too would shortly depart. It was the first of October, an ominous day according to the locals, but I felt no fear. In fact, I felt nothing but relief. I did not realize how much I needed a break from the hectic demands of the Leaf Academy. True, there were a few reports to finish and some light duties to attend to, but I imagined the next month would be restful for both young Ollie and me. First order of business? Write to his parents immediately. The boy was not forthcoming with the details of their delay, but I must have a timeline. I would need to plan for our food and other necessities. But for how long?

"How does walking suit you, young man? I thought we could explore the trail behind the academy. I think that red fox is running around again."

For the first time in a long while, I saw a glimmer of a smile on the boy's face. It was brief, but I was glad to see it. "And I secreted a few more apples. I have them in my pouch. We can take them with us, in case we get hungry. How does that sound?"

"Do red foxes eat apples?"

"No, I do not think they do. I think they prefer mice and rabbits."

"Oh," he said, looking a little sad.

"Come now, don't look so glum. Maybe this fox likes apples. We shall soon find out." We tied on our shoes, and I allowed the boy to carry the bag of apples. I stuffed my sketchpad and pencils in my satchel, along with a canteen of water and a few crackers. I did not think we would be gone too long, but one could never tell. I had a tendency to daydream; it had been so long since I could allow my mind to wander. Still, I had to look out for the boy. He was so fragile and would likely need comfort and companionship. Yes, this had been the right thing. We needed this quiet and solitude, both of us, for different reasons.

We walked out of the room, and by habit I locked it with my key. To my surprise, Ollie put his hand in mine as we headed down the stairs and outdoors. As we were not in school and there was no stern headmaster present to disapprove of such fatherly affection, I gladly accepted the boy's hand. I had never been a father, but I could not imagine a situation where I would not bring my son home for his holiday. How could a good man do such a thing? I quietly pledged to scold his father and remind him of his responsibilities. If it had been me, I would have moved heaven and earth to bring my son home.

But I was no father, nor would I ever be, I imagined. I released the boy's hand as we stepped out into the sunshine and smiled at the sight of the nodding green grass that blew in a pleasant breeze. There were songbirds nearby too, and I thought I could hear the water splashing in the creek. That was cer-

tainly just my imagination; I had never heard the water from this distance before. You had to travel
through the gate and down the path a little before
you could hear the creek. But I could hear it very
clearly now. I felt my skin prickle with strange
awareness. And just like that, all that was peaceful
and wonderful vanished.

A man stood at the far side of the yard just beyond
the metal fence. He stood stock-still like some kind
of menacing statue. I could not see his face or any of
his features, for it appeared to me that he was made
entirely of shadow. I heard Ollie's breathing still beside me. He must see him too! I shoved the boy behind me as I watched the shadow darken slightly and
then vanish altogether. I realized that I had been
holding my breath. Ollie was clutching the back of
my jacket.

"It's okay, Ollie. It was a trick of the light. See? There
is no one there." I pointed and smiled down at him.
Was I trying to convince Ollie or myself? There had
certainly been someone there. Yes, indeed. Probably
my height, maybe a little taller. He wore no hat and
had thick, dark hair.

"Let us go this way. There are many things to see on
the front lawn."

"But what about the red fox?"

"Surely we will find him there. Let us hunt for him."

"Okay," he agreed happily. He scampered in front of me while I looked behind us once more. No more shadow. Nothing at all. But he had been there.

All the hopefulness of the day blew away with the fear that overwhelmed me. For Ollie's sake, I continued on with our plan. Otherwise, I might very well have returned to my room to survey the grounds from my window, to look for the shadowy stranger from a safer vantage point.

To my surprise, we did find animal tracks. Many, many animal tracks. Even some that might be attributed to a dog or a red fox, as young Mr. LeFlore wanted to believe. Around lunchtime, we gobbled up the apples and drank our fill from the water canteen, and I decided it was time to return to the academy. For some reason, the thought of returning did not fill me with comfort even though I had many books to read and certainly could find much to entertain myself and my unexpected guest.

However, the idea of remaining outside disturbed me more. True, it was still early in the afternoon, but it was the first of October and the shadows seemed unusually long. When I turned my head slightly, I could see them moving in ways I had never seen before. Once or twice I caught Ollie looking around too, but neither of us admitted there was anything to fear. The boy found track after track, discovering one thing and then another. He even found a black feather and brought me to see it.

"You could add this to your collection," he said as he smiled sweetly.

How could he know that? He had not seen me hide the feather earlier. Or had he? A sick feeling washed over me. Must be all the apples. "We should leave it here, Ollie. Come, let's go inside now. I think it might rain."

The boy was quiet now. "You should take it. Add it to your collection, Mr. McCandlish," he said as he sidled closer and took my hand. Why did he feel so cold?

"No, thank you, Ollie. We should go inside now. We could drown in the rain, lad."

He snatched his hand away and stormed up the path to the school. I could not understand his behavior, but I was ready to be away from this horrible place. No, rain wasn't far away. I could smell it in the air. And what a rain it would be. We raced up the back steps just as the first drops splashed down. I closed the door behind us and locked it in case our unwanted guest attempted to come closer.

Yes, the shadow. I know I saw him.

Certainly, he would not try to come in. But if he did, I would defend myself and my charge. The rain fell harder, and by the time we reached my room it was coming down as if someone were tossing buckets of tears down from heaven, as my Nanna would have described it. Strange that I would think of her now.

"Come on, Ollie. Let us rest a bit and then think about what to cook for dinner." As we hurried down the corridor, I could see that my door was standing wide open. Ollie's hand was in mine again. *Ach, Hugh. He is nothing but a scared lad. Have a care and be kind. Would it have hurt to pick up the blooming feather?* I patted his hand once and went to investigate the open door, but he pulled me back with a surprising strength.

"They are here now, Mr. McCandlish. They have been watching us all day. We have to leave. You have to take me with you."

"We aren't going anywhere, Ollie. Stay put." I eased his small frame against the wall and dug in my satchel for the paring knife I carried for peeling the apples. It felt sticky from the juice, but I clutched it as determinedly as if it were the sword Excalibur. As I stepped closer, I saw the door was only partially open. I pushed it open all the way, but there was no one there. No one at all. No shadows, no interlopers.

Nothing but one black feather.

Chapter Five—Jocelyn

Although I felt unsettled now, my feelings weren't evidence of the paranormal. I wanted this; I'd been writing for months, hoping to get in here. And now here I was at the famed Leaf Academy freaking out over a few feathers. I focused on breathing as I closed my eyes and played back the audio recorders, both the one from the window and the one I carried with me downstairs. I was particularly interested to hear anything from this room or the hallway downstairs. There! I clicked the button and rewound it. Turning up the volume, I shoved my headphones into the plug with shaking fingers.

...me...

Someone was definitely making contact, but the phrase wasn't clear. The voice sounded like a child, maybe a boy? It was hard to tell with child spirits sometimes. I played it again.

...come find me...

And the voice was followed by a series of clicks. Familiar clicks like the ones my camera made. The camera! I'd forgotten to check my camera! I grabbed it and removed the memory card. As I sat on my makeshift bed, I opened my laptop and slid the card into the slot. A folder of pictures appeared, and I knew I would need to study each of them slowly. It was dark now, so dark that I had to pause to flip on my LED lamp. I shut the door while I was up. I had

M.L. Bullock

42

the feeling that at any moment someone would walk into the room. It seemed kind of silly closing the door on a ghost, but hey, it made me feel better. At least for a little while.

Sitting back on the cot, I hit play. The first photo freaked me out. This was a picture of me! I was leaving the room. There were several shots of me and then the closed door. If that wasn't freaky enough, I saw what looked like a face peering back at me from the shadowy corner of this very room. A little boy, if I had to guess, but the way he was turned, I could not see him full on. It was as if he did not want me to take his photo and turned away a little. But I could see the shape of his head, an ear and his profile. I caught my breath and immediately sent a copy of the picture to Midas along with a quick email.

Already seeing results. Wish me luck.

I closed the laptop before I could read what he wrote back. I didn't want to get into a long conversation or be reminded of the downside to investigating alone, but I had to show someone. I was getting evidence, good evidence. The kind I could believe in and rely on. Or maybe I just wanted to prove something to him. Or myself.

I heard a sound in the hallway. "Hello?" I hurried to the doorway and swore I heard footsteps run down the hall. My plan had been to take a nap and then investigate until sunup, but it looked like my plans might be changing. If the ghosties wanted to come out and play, I was game. I leaned against the door with my ear pressed against it. Yeah, footsteps retreating now. The sound was so real I could hear the grit beneath my visitor's shoes. Was this a real person? I mean, a living person? I opened the door and practically launched myself into the hallway.

I caught sight of a pant leg and a black shoe disappearing into another room. That was no child! There was someone here! I raced back to my room and grabbed my flashlight and camera. I wasn't sure what I would do with that combination, maybe blind the guy and then take his picture, but it was all I had. Why would someone in dress pants and dress shoes be hiding up here in the deserted Leaf Academy?

"Hey, I saw you!" I called as I waved my flashlight around. "You may as well come out." I paused in the hallway outside the room that I believed my unwanted guest had disappeared into. A cluster of shadows on the wall beside me fluttered and moved out of my view. Some shadows remained, silhouettes of the tree branches outside, but there had been more shadows before that. It was as if things that imitated shadows had been hiding amongst the real ones. And I saw them move! I had never seen anything like that before. They scurried across the wall and vanished to the opposite side where I couldn't see them. Now what?

I wished I'd thought to bring a K2 meter, but did I really need one? Strange crap was obviously going down at the Leaf Academy, and I was slap-dab in the middle of it. To say I didn't enjoy the adrenaline rush would be a lie, but I was no fool. People who hide out in deserted schools aren't exactly the cream of the social crop. I heard footsteps again and decided to follow the sound, not from the room this time but farther down. I walked down the hall a little slower now, waving my flashlight wildly as if at any moment the man would come running out to challenge me.

Or that pack of wild shadows.

Okay, this felt weird. The door to the next room was standing open, just like the front door had been. Like a crazy invitation from someone who desperately wanted to connect with me. Maybe that's what all this was? An attempt to connect? I had certainly heard that little boy's voice on the recorder. Maybe the guy in the dress pants was a ghost too? Sometimes apparitions could look like regular folks if you weren't paying attention.

"Hello? I thought I saw you come in here. Are you with the little boy? What is your name?" I flipped the camera to video and began to film as I walked into the room. There was no one here and nowhere for anyone to hide. The remnants of an old bed frame were in the corner of the room. There was a closet with no door and a broken window with glass on the floor. Oh yeah, that could be dangerous.

The only interesting thing was a wooden crate. I continued to film as I removed the lid and set it to the side. It was almost too heavy to move with one hand. Inside were lots of old books. I picked one up and scanned the title; it was something in Latin that I would never be able to translate without some help from the internet.

I took pictures of the book, inside and out. Then I reached inside the box and took out the next book. It was dusty with a worn fabric cover. "Journal" was written on the front cover in faded letters. There was handwriting inside, but it was too faded to read without proper lighting. I checked out the other books too. Just some school books, academic studies, nothing helpful at all. But this journal, it might give me some clues about the children and teachers here, many of whom called this place home for a time. I picked up the book and headed back to the hallway.

"If you brought me here to find this book, thank you. I am staying at the end of the hall if you want to visit me. But no touching. I will be waiting."

I walked back to my room anxious to examine the book. There were no more strange shadow for-mations, no more footsteps. Things had gotten quiet, and this would be a good time to catch forty winks. As I entered the room, I closed the door behind me again. Although I meant what I said about being open to visits, I liked to set boundaries early on. It was the same for the living and the dead with me. You could come this close but not much closer. For some reason, I thought about Sherman. I missed him.

Missed hearing his toenails clicking on the floor. Missed hearing him huff as he flopped down beside me.

Huh, I do miss him. Wow, that's a first.

"I'm in here if you want to talk to me, but please knock, okay?" I sat on my cot and took off my shoes but kept them close and left my socks on. It was too grungy in here to have any part of my body exposed to the elements or these surfaces. Before I dug into my newfound journal, I flipped through my own scrapbook. I'd been gathering stories about this place for months. First about the murder in 1937, the poor schoolteacher killed on the bottom floor. Then the second murder a few years later, similar to the first. Another teacher stabbed to death in his room in 1942. They found the body of a maintenance man hanging from a beam in the kitchen in 1950. Someone tried to open this place in the late seventies as a kind of local museum, but that hadn't worked out...no murders had been reported, just a suspicious death, but I couldn't get the man's name.

People believed that this place was cursed because the deaths all happened in October. And there was a fabulous legend about the October People. If you believed the stories, a ghostly swarm invaded this place during the month of October, but I didn't really believe that. What kind of ghost keeps up with the calendar? And why this particular month? Why not December? Yeah, spooky story, but it couldn't be true. Could it? It was October now...

Way to go, Jocelyn. Give yourself the heebie-jeebies before your nap. You'll be dead tired later. I snacked on a protein bar and picked up the old journal. With a flashlight, I scrutinized the name scribbled on the front page.

Oh my goodness! I recognized that name. This journal belonged to Moriah Mitchell, a former headmaster of the Leaf Academy. He was a man who by all accounts ruled with an iron fist and who went on to teach at one of the universities in Florida. He was here for the first murder. I couldn't wait to read what he had to say about this place. But as I strained to see the writing and blinked at the tiny script, I grew tired.

And sleep came far too easily.

Chapter Six—Jocelyn

I must have been dreaming about something crazy because I woke up in a cold sweat and my room was ice cold. The temperature must have dropped twenty degrees since I fell asleep. I slung back the sleeping bag. My watch was vibrating on my wrist; I loved the alarm app on this thing. Yep, it was a quarter past ten. Time to do the work. I sipped on some water, but not too much. There were no working "facilities" in this place, so if I did have to go, it would be in the woods. Yeah, I planned on holding it until the sun came up, so sipping, no downing a whole bottle.

The wood popped a few times, which I chalked up to old boards contracting from the colder temperatures. That happened in old buildings like this one. The façade and columns were brick, but inside this place was wood and more wood from wall panels to floors. Almost every step you took, the floor creaked beneath you. And as I swapped out batteries in the camera in the hallway, I paused to listen. I didn't detect any sounds, but the place had an "opening night" feel to it. Like there were many people outside the building just dying to get in.

Great terminology, girl.

And I knew all about opening night. I had been a drama major before I fell in love with photography. I always got cast in the strangest roles. I played La Sorcière Blanche in some play with a title that escaped my memory now. Later I played the Cowardly Lion in an all-female production of The Oz Story, which I loved. Those were the two most memorable, but I had been on stage at least a dozen times in various roles, and that's what tonight reminded me of. Not because I would be investigating the auditorium either. That couldn't be it. No, it was something else. Opening nights came with a strange kind of excitement, like what I was feeling now.

Yeah, you're a weirdo, Jocelyn.

I swapped out the digital cards in the cameras and replaced them with fresh ones, just in case I needed the digital space. I would hate to miss anything. I'd walked this floor already and planned to do so again, but now it was time to target the auditorium. I would set this rig up in there. It had a handy setting that would snap photos only if something moved. I tapped on the screen and set it for the highest sensitivity setting too. That way, any change in light patterns or shadow patterns would trigger the camera. I had a K2 on my hip, along with an audio recorder in my pocket, and my handheld camera dangled from the strap around my neck. My dreads felt itchy and I needed a shower, but hey, this was the life, right?

I shuffled down the stairs and to my amazement heard a few notes of piano music, but it only lasted a moment. Was there a piano on this floor? It was certainly possible. I hadn't walked through the auditorium yet, and that would be an obvious location for such an instrument. The K2 on my hip began to bleep as I cleared the last step. I stood in the foyer now, near the headmaster's office. To my right was a long corridor and the auditorium; to my left were presumably just classrooms. No time like the present. I set the camera and tripod case down and waved the K2 smoothly at waist height. Point two, point seven...wow! What a jump! It was high to my left and normal to my right. I decided to put off my auditorium visit and follow this surge to see where it would lead me. I reached for my digital recorder and clicked it on.

"Hey, is that you? My name is Jocelyn. What is your name?"

Name...

I gulped at the sound of a deep, gruff voice that I could plainly hear with my own ears. Was it mocking me?

"I said, what is your name?"

Said...

"Is that all you can do? Is that how you get your kicks, mocking people?" I frowned as the K2 went still. Nothing now. I walked a few feet farther down the hall, but it was useless. No spikes now. Dead as a doornail.

"Hey, where did you go? You could at least tell me your name."

Silence met me. With a sigh, I continued my walk down the dark corridor. Man, it was dark, like walking in a tunnel underground. I flicked on my flashlight so I could avoid tripping over random junk. In the foyer, light streamed in from the window over the landing. Here in this corridor, though, there seemed to be an absence of light. Very odd indeed.

Most of the doors were open, so I peeked inside each room but didn't detect a thing on the K2. I headed back to the foyer to gather my things and continue on my mission, but my tripod case was missing.

"What the frick?" I said as I glanced around. Could I have dropped it off somewhere else? No, I knew for a fact I had it with me, along with the camera case. I set them both down here and then followed that spike and...

Oh my God. How in the hell did that happen?

I was looking down the opposite corridor, the one that led to the auditorium, and I could plainly see the tripod. It was out of its case and extended fully, just like I would have set it up if I had not been distracted by some mischievous spirit. I shoved the digital recorder in my pocket and grabbed my camera case. I couldn't turn back now; someone was expecting me. I headed down the hall. Yeah, that was my tripod. Despite my curiosity, seeing my things moved without the help of human hands unsettled me. I remembered to control my breathing and reminded myself that this was why I had come here. I wanted to see this stuff, right?

"Thank you," I said to the air around me. "But let's go in, shall we?" With clumsy hands, I opened the door and dragged my case and tripod inside. Man, the smell. It smelled like rot. Thankfully, not dead animal rot but certainly wood and leaves. And oh yeah, there was a hole in the wall and the ceiling. How did that happen? Was that a tree branch hanging down? This place sure needed some tender loving care. There were rows upon rows of theater chairs, all light-colored wood that must have been very fine once upon a time. Looking back at the door I just walked through, I was amazed at the sight of the massive doorframe surrounded by wide, dark wood panels. The ceiling was high, really high. I waved my flashlight around and immediately spotted a few small openings up there too. That was weird. The auditorium must extend out some because I was looking up at a starry sky, not the bottom of the top floor.

Interesting.

The walls were covered with moldy once-white plaster panels, and each of those was surrounded by yellowed wood that might have been painted gold. They were like neat boxes, or they would have been if the paint wasn't flaking and the plaster wasn't rotting off the walls. Looking ahead, I couldn't see a clear path to the stage. Some of the chairs were overturned, another oddity since they were connected in clusters of six. Had someone turned over the entire row? No, make it three rows. I guess so. Who would do that? Vandals?

"Hello?" I said more quietly than I'd intended. *Don't be timid, Jocelyn. You'd better show them who's boss.* "My name is Jocelyn Graves," I said a bit more confidently. "I came to see you in the play. Are you performing tonight?" I stepped around the dumped-over chairs and found a space in the center aisle to place the tripod. I took the camera out of the case and set it up, double-checking the settings. Yep, still set to high sensitivity. I hit the wide-angle option to give myself a better shot at capturing anything that crossed that stage.

"I hear you like to perform in the month of October, and I'm excited to see your show. I haven't seen a good play in a while." I waved the K2 around but got only a random blip or two. I kept rolling with the audio recorder. I would have liked to sit down to rest, but none of these chairs looked remotely clean. Instead, I paced the outer aisles hoping to get some action. I kept my eyes and my flashlight trained on the stage.

"Hello? Why are you hiding? I can see you."

Peeking out from behind a faded crimson curtain, a pale face looked back at me, but only for the briefest of seconds. No! There he was again. It was the face of a boy! Okay, was I talking myself into seeing that, or did I actually see a ghost boy? To be fair, he did look similar to the boy I'd caught in the image upstairs.

"Hello?" I said in a whisper, but he did not reappear. I carefully made my way to the stage.

Chapter Seven—Hugh

I woke up to a horrible sound. Someone was banging on my door. Furiously banging. No, that wasn't it. It was my bed, my very own bed that was banging, shaking about as if some invisible giant had every intention of tossing me out of it. I screamed as I clung to the wobbly headboard and then everything got still.

"Ollie!" I whispered once my heart began to beat at a steady rate again. How could the boy sleep through such an event? "Ollie, are you all right, lad?"

I blindly reached for the lamp on the night table. I found the screw that flipped the light on and twisted it. Nothing. No light at all. Had the electrical service gone down? That would be no surprise; it was still raining from what I could hear, and the electrical often went out during rainstorms. There were no lights on in the hallway, I noted as I scurried to the door to open it. The floor was cold beneath my feet. I searched the boy's cot, but it was empty. Where could he have gone? Had he heard or seen my bed shaking and fled the room in fear? What was happening here? I peered at my bed in the darkness as I rubbed my eyes; clearly, the bed was not resting in the spot it should be in. The footboard was almost a half-foot from the wall. I shoved it into place and slid my feet into my slippers as I pulled on my robe. There was certainly no heat; it was unbearably cold. Where could the boy have gone? To find a warm fireplace? One of Nanna's sayings came to mind, but I did not have the heart to speak it aloud.

Cold as the grave, Hugh. Cold as the grave, dear lad.

Strange goings-on here at the Leaf Academy. Too strange. I checked under the bed briefly, but there was no obvious cause for the violence I had endured. I hurried out into the hallway in search of the boy. He was my responsibility after all. Poor, helpless boy. Imagine leaving him in the care of a stranger?

"Ollie? Ollie LeFlore? Where are you hiding?"

I heard footsteps walking down the staircase. "Ollie? Don't make me chase you in the dark, young man. Ollie?"

Then I heard the sounds of laughter and tinkling glass, as if someone were having a party on the bottom floor. Near the auditorium. No, the sounds were coming from inside the auditorium. And a piano played a lively tune, something sweet and familiar. What was that tune? I knew it but could not recall the name.

As I stepped onto the bottom floor, the power must have been restored, for every light in the place came on. I gripped the newel post and held on while a wave of confusion struck me. I shook my head and rubbed my face with my hand. Yes, I was alive, but was I awake? I rubbed at my skin roughly to wake myself up. I could feel stubble on my face; I needed a shave. I was sweating and in need of a shower to refresh myself. A woman passed me wearing a long red dress and carrying a slender red rose in her hand. She looked so familiar, but I could not place her. Was there a party going on here? Was that why the headmaster had been so insistent that I leave?

Perhaps this was the true reason for the dismissal of the staff for a month. Merrymaking. But who were these people? Yes, there were many people here; they were filing in through the open doors of the academy. And they all knew me, for many of them greeted me. An older woman in a black and gray dress purred my name as she passed me on her way into the auditorium. She too was familiar. A swell of music indicated that the performance was about to begin. Someone said my name again.

Hugh McCandlish! Come sit with me.

The woman in red appeared in the doorway. She wiggled her finger at me as if to summon me to her, but I could not see her face and was not willing to obey her. Emma? The kitchen girl?

"What is all this?" I asked, feeling embarrassed to be walking through the middle of a fine party in my pajamas and robe. What would they think? Why was I here again? Oh, yes. Ollie. The poor lad. I had to find him.

"Leave him to us," a man said. He was about as tall as me but with long, jet-black hair, and he wore strange garb.

Was I going mad? *No, that's not it. I know who I am and where I am. I am not mad. I am Hugh McCandlish. I am a teacher here, and this is the Leaf Academy.* But where was Ollie?

"Leave him with us. He belongs with us," the man said again as he bumped my shoulder with his. He shoved me hard and walked into the auditorium. Was that a threat? Was this stranger threatening me?

Others began to appear in the hallway. I could see them now, yes. I could see them very clearly. A very thin woman, with her hair in two long braids over her shoulders. She looked very much like Mrs. Smith, but certainly that could not be. Was this a costume party? She wore a deerskin dress and leggings. She was whispering words I could not understand; she was speaking a different language! Oh, dear. I was not proficient with languages at all.

"I don't understand you. Speak slower, perhaps." But she walked away and headed to the auditorium. And that's when I heard him scream.

Ollie was screaming my name.

I ran as fast as I could into the auditorium, but my hasty pursuit of Ollie was delayed when the place went black. It was so black I could not see my hand in front of my face. The lights were gone again, but no, that couldn't be right. I could see the many faces around me. They glowed slightly in the darkness; they were not like before, real people with friendly expressions. The absence of light revealed their true nature; they were surely not of this world. *The October People!*

And they all hated me. They wanted me to die!

I ran past them into the auditorium screaming Ollie's name. The stage was empty except for the little boy curled into a ball in the center of it. His hair was mussed, the dark strands covering his face, and he was heaving as if he had been crying for a long while.

"Hush, now. I have you, Ollie." I pulled the boy close and collected him quickly as he shivered in my arms. Poor child. What was going on in this place? I hesitated on the stage wondering whether to go left or right or what to do. From somewhere in the darkness, I heard a man clapping; yes, it had to be a man's hands. They were loud, and then many hands were clapping. The sound was thunderous. And then silence. I raced from the auditorium as lightning filled the hall with a strange blue light. The faces vanished, and I began to cry as I ran with Ollie in my arms, his head on my chest. He was crying too.

We would leave this place come morning, as soon as we could navigate the road. Perhaps the rain would stop by then. We would leave the Leaf Academy and never come back. This place truly was cursed; it was the home of the damned. Mrs. Smith had been right all along, but then again, she was one of them.

This place belonged to the October People—it had always been theirs.

I hurried down the long corridor and raced to my room, holding Ollie as he wept. I lied to him, "It will be all right, lad. It will be all right. We will leave this place when the sun comes up. I promise you. I do so promise. Do you hear me?"

"Yes," he sniffled, but he did not let me go. I did not have the heart to ask him what happened. How did he end up in the auditorium? What devil had led him there and why? Some questions need not be asked or answered. There would be time for that later. Yes, later. At least it had stopped raining.

After a while, I laid him on his cot and pulled the covers around him tightly. I locked the door this time, so he could not walk away in his sleep and so no one could enter. I sat at my desk a good long while. I heard music downstairs and more than once heard feet running past my door, but nobody knocked. I heard no voices. Not like before.

But they were here. They were just waiting for us to step outside into the darkness. But I would not do such a thing. I would not.

I waited for the sun to come up. It was nearly four—it wouldn't be long now, but I felt so tired. So very tired. I decided to lie in my bed, not to sleep but only to rest and wait and watch over Ollie. I shoved my hand under the pillow to plump it up a bit when my fingers brushed against something strange.

I pulled out a long black feather. How had this gotten here? It wasn't here before. It couldn't have been. But it was here now.

I glanced down at Ollie, who was sound asleep now. A brief beam of moonlight passed his face; the light was quickly spirited away by yet another cloud. But during those few seconds I could swear by all the saints above that I saw a smile on the boy's face.

I flung the feather on the floor and stared at Ollie. I was unable to look away now. I stared until the sun rose and the sounds downstairs faded.

And when all was quiet, I fell asleep.

Chapter Eight—Jocelyn

I hung around the auditorium for an hour, but the boy's face never reappeared. I prayed that the camera had captured something. "Please don't tear up my equipment while I'm gone," I said to whoever might be listening. Geesh, how cold was it now? My phone app said 52 degrees Fahrenheit, but I could see my breath.

Wait, that wasn't my breath. It was someone else's, and they were standing beside me. Someone much shorter and invisible. I didn't move but watched the tiny clouds of breath appear and disappear, and they were getting farther away. He was leaving the auditorium! Could this be the boy I saw?

"Hey, wait!" I said, but the tiny puffs of frosty air disappeared and reappeared, each time a little farther away. I ran out into the hall, but there was no trace of anyone or anything remotely like what I saw. He was leading me somewhere, but where?

You know where, Jocelyn Graves. Back to your room. He likes it in there.

I hurried up the stairs, but it was impossible to be quiet. I don't know why I bothered trying. The entity or entities that lived here already knew I was here. Maybe I was afraid to draw more attention to myself. I couldn't say. Then I heard my phone ring. But I turned the ringer off...that's not right. I raced down the hall and dug in my bag to find it. The phone was glowing, and the ringtone brought me some comfort. It was hard to be afraid when your favorite pop singer was singing about being "happy."

"Hello?" I said a little too desperately. What time was it anyway? I glanced at my watch. Was it seven o'clock already? Yeah, sure enough. I could see the sun coming over the forest at the back of the house. How was it I was losing track of time here? I wasn't usually this off-schedule.

"Hi, Miss Graves? This is Melissa with Happy Paws."

"Oh no, is it Sherman? Is he hurt?"

"He's not hurt, but he refuses to eat or drink anything. He doesn't act as if he feels well. I was wondering, is your dog on any kind of medication? Or does he have a condition that we need to be aware of? Maybe something you forgot to list on his paperwork?"

"Condition? Is Sherman okay?"

"Well, I'm not sure. That's why I'm calling. Some dogs don't do well in boarding situations, and Sherman is clearly one of those dogs." She didn't sound upset, but I could hear the genuine concern in her voice.

"He hasn't hurt anyone, has he? He's never been aggressive with me. Never."

She answered in a kind voice, "No, nothing like that. He's moping, not going out, not eating. He might be sick, and if he is, he shouldn't be around our other visitors. I hope you understand. You will have to come get him or send someone."

"Uh, okay. I'm not far away. I will come get him, Melissa. Thanks for the call."

I could hear the sympathy in her voice. "I hate to cut Sherman's stay short since he's such a sweet boy, but we have to be safe."

"All right, I'll be there soon."

"Great, thanks. Sorry again to have to call you."

"No, it's fine. Tell my puppy I'm on the way."

I hung up the phone and paced the room briefly. Okay, change of plans. I'd never worked on a paranormal investigation with a dog before, but it didn't look like I had much of a choice. I only had to stay one more night...surely Sherman and I would be okay. Unless he really was sick. I guess I had to play it by ear. I hated to kill a few precious hours, but Sherman came first.

I grabbed my purse and keys. I'd go pick up Sherman, and then the order of business would be to find food and a public restroom, review some of the evidence and continue the investigation. This would be my last night here at the Leaf Academy. Last night, last chance to see something truly paranormal...although

I couldn't imagine how I could top what I had already seen.

Strange, I don't remember laying that feather on my purse. Boy, this bird couldn't keep his feathers, could he? Although I didn't want to, I picked up the feather and set the thing in the windowsill. I'd check it out further when I got back. As I headed out of the room, I stepped into the hall and again caught a glimpse of a pair of legs.

What the heck, man?

I ran to the far end of the corridor and distinctly heard the sound of keys jingling. *Damn it! Nobody is supposed to be here but me!* I opened the door, a door I missed earlier, and ran up a narrow set of metal stairs that led to the roof. Without thinking about the holes I saw earlier, I ran a few feet and then paused.

Yes, there was someone up here, a guy with dark hair, and he was smoking a cigarette. What should I do? Run back down the stairs? Hunker down and hide?

"Hey," he said as he flicked the butt off the side of the building. The sun was up now and cast a golden light on his somewhat handsome face. He looked like a biking enthusiast, the Harley-Davidson kind—from the 1950s. He had on blue jeans with rolled cuffs, a black leather jacket and a white t-shirt. Well, it was sort of white. My sixth sense was screaming at me,

"Run, idiot!" but I was fascinated and terrified. Too terrified to do anything like run.

Weapons, weapons. What kind of weapons do I have? None. None at all. Just keep your cool, Jocelyn, and stay away from the edge of the building.

He walked a little closer to me as he shook another cigarette out of the pack that he pulled from his jacket pocket. He offered me one, but I shook my head emphatically.

"No, thanks."

"Not a smoker, huh? Probably smart. Smarter than me."

"I don't think you're supposed to be here, mister. This is private property."

He grinned and showed brown stained teeth. Gross. "And yet, here you are, little lady. Here we both are. Probably for very much the same reasons."

Oh, he must be a paranormal investigator. I breathed a sigh of relief but didn't let my guard down yet. Not completely.

"You come here often?" I asked stupidly. He laughed, and I shook my head at my poorly chosen question. "I mean, have you been here before?"

"Many times." He lit his smoke, and the smell of tobacco wafted in my direction. "Many times."

"I see." I shifted my position but didn't try to get any closer. He really needed to go. I couldn't do a proper investigation with this guy wandering around the building. I was just trying to figure out how to ask him to get lost, in a polite way, when he asked me the strangest question.

"Are you human?"

"What?" I clutched my purse tighter as the coldest sensation I ever experienced crept from my head clear down to my feet. I was completely encased in cold clamminess. I didn't think it was a funny question, but for some reason I laughed. "Yeah, I am human."

He sat down on a broken chair and appeared to be somewhat relieved at my answer. "Thank God. I hate it when they aren't human."

I didn't know what to say to that, so I didn't say anything for a while. But time was not on my side. Sherman was waiting for me, and the clock was ticking on my investigation.

"What if I wasn't?"

His eyes bored into me, and he stood back up. He wasn't menacing exactly, but he didn't look like a happy camper. *Damn it, Jocelyn. You and your big mouth.* "Why do you ask?"

"I just think it's odd, you wondering if I'm human. What if I wasn't? What would you have done about it?"

"I would have to kill you, of course. Kill you and peel your skin off."

With a deep, guttural scream erupting from my lips, I let fear fuel me as I jetted back down the narrow stairs and then the two flights of stairs inside the building. I raced out the front door, fumbling briefly for the key, and then somehow made it to my car.

"Holy crap!" I repeated over and over as I put the key in the ignition and slung the car in reverse. I didn't stop until I got to the end of the driveway and then patted my hands on the steering wheel to steady myself.

What the hell was that? That wasn't a person. No way was that a person. That was something else entirely. No living person had ever scared me so much in my life.

And that was saying something.

Chapter Nine—Jocelyn

By the time I made it back to Happy Paws, I wasn't swearing or gasping for air. Whoever that guy was, his intention was clear—he wanted to scare the hell out of me. Mission accomplished, dude, but I wasn't going to sit around crying. I put in a phone call to the realtor and waited to hear something back from her. Somebody besides me needed to know some weird biker dude threatened to kill me and peel my skin off. I shivered again at the memory of his cigarette glowing and his eyes narrowing evilly. There hadn't been a shadow of a smile on his face. And that was nothing to joke about, anyway.

"I'm here for Sherman. I'm his..."

"Right, you're his Mom. I'll go get him. Sorry it didn't work out." The girl disappeared into the back and returned with my dog and his overnight bag. He immediately began wagging his tail and practically dragged her to me. "Wow! This is the happiest he's been since he got here. Sorry again. If you have to leave again, maybe next time we can try those treats, the kind that help dogs relax. That helps with some of our visitors."

I didn't like that idea at all. I never took meds and sure wouldn't pass them off to my dog. I smiled politely and signed Sherman out. We headed back to the car, ran a few errands and poked around until my phone rang.

"Hey, Adrian, thanks for calling me back so soon."

"No problem. How can I help you?"

I glanced at Sherman in the rearview mirror. He was sitting patiently in the backseat, just happy to be hanging out with his "Mom." He didn't look sick at all to me. Wow, I was a mom. How hilarious was that? And with that realization, all the weirdness I experienced earlier seemed like a dream. "I just want to verify that no one else has been given permission to be at the Leaf Academy. Not at the same time as me, I mean."

"There is only one key, and you have it. Is everything okay? Should I be concerned?"

"No, but I did see someone in there. A man was on the roof, and I think he was inside a few times."

Adrian paused and asked, "What did he look like? Did you call the police?"

"No, I didn't because, well, that would kind of defeat the purpose. I don't want to get the police involved unless I have to. I've seen vagrants in deserted buildings before, but this guy was a bit odd. I just thought someone should know about him." I tried to laugh it off. I felt stupid now calling Adrian over a weirdo. But she didn't seem surprised at all.

She sighed and said, "I should have told you this before, but Mr. Holloway didn't want to influence your investigation. There have been reports over the years, many reports, as you well know, beyond just the rumors about some October curse."

"You mean the October People. I know what they say about the property. I mean, that's kind of why I am there. And I read all about the murders, the one in the thirties and then the two others."

Adrian cleared her throat. "Um, there are more than those. Not necessarily murders but two suicides and several disappearances."

"Oh," I said as I sipped water from my bottle.

"Tell me, Jocelyn, what did this vagrant look like? Did he have black hair? Was he wearing a motorcycle jacket?"

I blinked at hearing her question. "Um, a motorcycle jacket. How did you know? You've had dealings with this guy before? I mean, is he dangerous?"

"He's dead. That's Mr. Holloway's brother. He killed himself there, threw himself off that roof in 1957. That's why Mr. Holloway closed the place. Gary was his older brother; it appears Gary never left. At least that's what Mr. Holloway believes."

"I didn't know. I'm sorry."

"I guess that means you're done with the investigation. Should I come by and get the key? Are you leaving now?" Adrian sounded a bit disappointed but not surprised. I was starting to get the feeling I wasn't the first paranormal investigator to spend time there. What were they hoping for? I was no exorcist, not by a long shot.

"I'm not leaving, Adrian. I just wanted to know about this guy. You know, as far as we know, he could be someone trying to pull a prank."

She blew into the phone as if she didn't believe me. "Who would go to the trouble of doing all that? I mean, just to scare someone? And from 1957 on to today? Even Mr. Holloway doesn't go in there. I think you were kind of his last hope. He wants to sell the place, get rid of the whole shebang, but how can he do that if it's infested with...bad memories? You have to know that's what he's been told. That the Leaf Academy is paranormally and permanently infested with activity. And it's getting worse."

"I think it's time you leveled with me, Adrian. I take it you didn't give me access because you liked my photos or my writing sample. What am I really doing there?"

She paused, and I heard the sound of a squeaking door on the phone. "We know about the ghosts, Jocelyn. It's not that we don't believe it, but we want it on record. And from someone credible, someone who would do their due diligence. I'll be honest, we're not sure what the next step would be, but you come highly recommended to us. Highly. If you want to call it off, we'd understand. I would understand; Mr. Holloway would understand. You couldn't pay me to walk in there, and I'm trying to sell the place for him. I think he just wants some peace. And I want to help him find it."

I chewed the inside of my lip. "What do you know about a little boy? Have any children died at the Leaf Academy? Maybe a former student?"

Adrian hesitated again. "Not that I know of, but you are not the first person to mention a ghost boy. Sightings have been going on for decades. The first murder victim, Mr. McCandlish—"

Suddenly my phone went dead and Sherman began to whine from the backseat. I pounded on the phone's keyboard, but nothing was happening. I plugged it into the charger, but not even that could breathe life into it.

I turned around in my seat to pet my dog. "Okay, boy. If I'm going to be your Mom and you're going to be my dog—I mean, kid—then you should know this is what life is like with me. I hunt ghosts. In fact, I'm going back now to find one. Possibly a very mean one. Are you in?"

Sherman licked my hand, which I took to mean yes. Not all the dots were connected, but my mission was much clearer than it had been: find out who this "boy" was and what he wanted. And show that creepy rooftop entity that I wasn't one to be pushed around.

I was feeling big and bad until I reached the driveway of the Leaf Academy. For some reason, it looked even weedier, if that was a word. I could see less of the house than before...were the trees trying to block my way?

Okay, October People. Ready or not, here we come.

Chapter Ten—Hugh

I woke up to a tickling sensation on my face. It was Ollie, rubbing that horrible black feather across my forehead. I swatted it away, relieved to see that the sun was still up and the door remained shut.

"Wake up. We have to go now. You promised."

I snatched the feather from his hand a bit more ferociously than I intended. He stepped back and out of my reach. Did the boy think I would hit him?

"Where did you get this feather, Ollie? Did you bring it up from the yard? Did you sneak out while I was sleeping?"

"No, I did not. It was on your pillow."

I swung my feet over the side of the bed. My head felt like I'd been at the tavern all night, an activity I had not participated in for at least ten years but certainly welcomed now. "The things you say, Ollie. We will go, but you and I must talk first." I rubbed my scruffy face with my hand. My stomach rumbled and my mouth was dry, but first things first. "Why were you in the auditorium last night?"

Ollie backed away another step. I noticed that he had dressed already. Suddenly I was overwhelmed with sickness. I could not shake the nausea that threatened to cripple me. After I closed my eyes a minute, I pressed Ollie for information. "Tell me about the auditorium last night. Who were those people? Why did you go there?"

Ollie's dark eyes welled up with tears. "What people? I heard music. I thought someone was here."

The boy was lying to me. He saw those people—the woman in the red dress, the one who looked like Emma, and the strange lady with the braids who looked so much like Mrs. Smith. The menacing shadow that hovered over the place. "If you heard music, you should have told me about it and not gone adventuring by yourself. It's not safe, Ollie." I dressed quickly as I thought about what to do next. If we set off by foot, we would walk about half a day before we came to the first residence. Surely they would help us. Too bad I had no car and no way to call for one...unless I broke into the headmaster's office, which I had every right to do. I was after all the de facto headmaster now, as I was here at the Leaf Academy caring for a student while Mr. Mitchell was on his way to Georgia for his extended vacation. Yes! There was certainly a phone in his office!

"You still haven't explained yourself. Why were you in the auditorium? Why?" I wanted to vomit, but my mouth felt dry, so very dry.

"I heard singing. I thought it was my mother. She likes to sing." He ducked his head and stared at his hands, a gesture that accompanied many a tall tale around the academy. But always from other children, never Ollie. So why was he lying now?

"Your parents are not coming, are they? Tell me the truth. Where are your parents?" He refused to speak to me. I struggled to my feet and put on my clothes. I was sliding my suspenders up over my shoulders when I caught a glimpse of the boy's cot. It was littered with pictures. I recognized the paper, the very expensive paper like the kind the headmaster liked to use. But there was no time to give lectures on thievery and asking permission. I could not take my eyes off the images; they were compelling in a ghastly way. I squatted down and picked them up, examining them one by one. There was a small boy standing on the auditorium stage. A dark figure behind him, with large, slanted eyes. And this was clearly the woman with the braids—and that strange man! Yes! Ollie had seen them too!

But the last picture, the one I now held in my trembling hands, disturbed me the most. Clearly, it was me. I recognized the beard; I usually kept it trimmed neat, but in this illustration I was unkempt. My suspenders were tangled around my arms, and I was dead. I had to be dead; I was lying in the center of the stage with a knife protruding from my chest.

"Ollie?" I asked, unable to formulate a question beyond that.

He put his hand on my shoulder. "We have to go now."

"Why would you draw this? This is a nasty thing to do, Ollie." And then my mind swirled with fear-fueled questions. "Did you kill that bird, lad? Tell me. Tell me the truth. You killed it, didn't you? I believed you were innocent—how could you do such a thing?"

"I did not, Mr. McCandlish! Please, sir. We have to go. They will be coming back soon, and they will be so angry." Ollie's voice shook, but I could not move from the spot. Nor could I stop staring at the illustration of my death.

"Why did you draw this? Don't lie to me, lad! You saw them; I can see by your own expression that you saw them just as I did!"

He took another step away from me, and this time his back was to the door. He fumbled with the button of his coat as he began to cry. "I drew them to show you what will happen if we stay! They're whispering to me, Mr. McCandlish! Whispering so loudly! Make them stop!"

I held the picture up and waved it at him. "What does this mean?"

"Please, we have to go."

And right before my eyes, two black, snakelike hands reached through the closed door and snatched the boy away. One hand was clamped around his mouth so he could not scream, and his eyes were wide with terror. Loud footsteps banged down the hallway, and then there was nothing.

Nothing except the sound of my own shouting.

After some time, I heaved myself off the floor, slid on my shoes and reached for the doorknob. There was nothing for it. I had to search for Ollie. Something had grabbed him, stolen him and spirited him away. But where had they taken him? This must be the work of those horrible creatures—the October People! I glanced down at the foreboding picture.

Did I really have to wonder? I knew where I would find him. I knew where I had to go. If I wanted to save Ollie, that is. Like a coward I paced the floor and considered, if only briefly, how quickly I could run from the place. How long would it take me to put a hundred miles between myself and this repulsive school? But how could I? Ollie trusted me like nobody ever had. If I had ever had a son, he would have been a boy like Ollie. Quiet, thoughtful. And now the lad was caught in this hideous tangle of events the same as me, yet I did not believe him to be the cause of any of it. What should I do?

I heard music. The tinkling of a piano, the sound of a woman's voice, a clear and elegant soprano. Without bothering to lock the door, I trudged into the hallway. I was never coming back, was I? There wasn't a chance I would be able to escape this place. Not with evil creatures lurking in the hallways, snatching children through doors, chasing us, their phantom footsteps always behind us.

As I opened the door and walked into the hall, I wondered how all this had come about. What had I done to deserve this? Was it some cosmic collusion that caused me to be here with Ollie? Was this always to be my fate? My only wish had been to see the star alignment, to enjoy the quiet beauty of the countryside. But that was before a helpless boy needed me.

I took another step and then another. I ignored the many shadowy faces that peered at me from inside the now open doors. And to think, Nanna always told us that spooks only appeared after dark, that they were creatures of the night. But here it was afternoon and they were everywhere. I got the sensation that somehow, the walls were writhing with them. Yes, the spooks were built into the place. They were ground into the bricks, and when the time was right, they sprang to life.

Nanna had been wrong. Golden sunshine filtered through the big window over the landing. I was not surprised to see people huddled together in the chairs; they were whispering to one another, and I was the subject of their conversation. They lined the stairs and waited for me on the lower level. But these weren't living people.

They were dead. And I was about to join them.

Chapter Eleven—Jocelyn

"We're in here, boy. This is where we'll sleep tonight. Or at least where you'll sleep." He made a funny groaning sound, and I laughed at hearing it. Sometimes I felt as if the dog knew what I was saying; more likely, he just understood the tone of my voice. I always knew dogs were smart, but I had no idea they were so expressive until I adopted Sherman.

After my encounter with the dead Gary Holloway, I had to admit that I was happy not to return to the Leaf Academy alone. I still wasn't sure what Adrian and Mr. Holloway expected me to accomplish, but here I was. Yeah, this was why I came, but those kinds of freaky encounters still shook me.

And he threatened to peel my skin off!

No matter how experienced you were, hearing something like that would rock a person. But no way was I skipping out on the Leaf Academy investigation. What I was going to do was take the next few hours to review the research material I brought with me and flip through the journal I found. I looked out the window for a few minutes, just in case Mr. Weirdo showed up again. Could that really have been Gary Holloway? If I had a picture to look at, I was sure I could identify him. I would never forget the clover-shaped mole on his cheek, the definite cowlick at his right temple. If he was really an apparition, he must be a strong one to project himself into our world with such detail.

It was still early in the day, only noon, but my time was running out. I should have asked for one more day; I was pretty sure Adrian would have given me the extra time. No, I better stick with the plan. I opened my soda and sniffed the air. I thought I caught a whiff of stale cigarette smoke, but then it was gone as quickly as I detected it. Sherman didn't move an inch; in fact, he decided my sleeping bag was the perfect place to lie down.

"I thought you were sick. I'm glad you're not, but what are you going to do when I have to really go out of town?" I shook my head at him as I opened the journal. With the combination of daylight and my LED light, I could finally read the name written neatly inside.

This journal belongs to Moriah Mitchell.

The first twenty pages or so were pretty mundane, the usual stuff one might read in a headmaster's journal. Kids behaving, kids misbehaving. Oh, this looked interesting.

I spoke with Mr. McCandlish today. He has seen the boy; the cycle continues. What was thought banished has returned. I fear that the worst will happen for him, but who can prevent it? I cannot. That I know as well as any here. There is no hope for it.

The pages felt dirty beneath my fingers, but I turned them hastily.

McCandlish calls the boy Ollie, and the ghost becomes more visible by the hour. It is God's blessing that many are gone now. McCandlish is fully entwined in the Spider's trap, for it has made itself known to the sad teacher in ways I could not have imagined. I depart this place today, and that is none too soon. I have warned McCandlish that he must not stay here, that he must leave. He will not listen. He will be gone when I return, I am sure of it. May God have mercy on us all!

A sketch of black feathers had been carefully drawn at the bottom of the page. It was actually very fine work from an artistic standpoint, but seeing the familiar image in this old journal gave me the creeps. How was it that I, a visitor to the Leaf Academy more than eighty years later, would see the same feather? But it couldn't be the same. There were probably lots of crows in this area and had been for quite some time. Lots and lots.

The journal stopped abruptly at the end of September 1937, but I kept flipping through the pages. Many pages had been torn out of the book; a few stubs were left, but clearly someone had very sloppily removed some of them. I skimmed the book again. Nope, those pages were gone.

"Come on, Sherman. Let's go down the hall for a second."

I returned to the room where I'd found the box that held the journal and sifted through it hoping to find more of the same. Most of the items were uninteresting, just as I first believed, but then I found an old red paper folder. Inside were the missing pages. These were drawings, a child's drawings by the look of them.

And they were terrible to look at.

A small boy sitting in a chair in the auditorium, a gruesome smile on his face. A dead man lying on the stage with a knife in his chest. A woman floating above him, her mouth open as if she were screaming or singing or saying something. And there were so many eyes, all around the boy and the stage. I took pictures of the horrible images because that was all I could think to do. A shudder shot through me as I slid the papers around and my eyes fell on the last sheet of paper.

This was me.

It had to be me. I was sitting next to the boy, and beside me was the man in the black jacket, the one I believed to be Gary Holloway. This was no Rembrandt painting, but the artist had enough skill for me to identify myself easily enough. My dreadlocks were hanging over my shoulders, a camera dangled from my neck—and my neck! Why was it hanging at such an odd angle?

Why did my neck look like that? Was it broken?

"No!" I said as I let the picture flutter to the ground. I heard the sound of an old-fashioned lighter clicking in the hallway. Sherman heard it too. He got quiet, but his eyes were focused on the open door. He wasn't sitting beside me now, as was his custom whenever I got still. No, the furry canine was poised to pounce, run or snap at the intruder. A shadow passed the door. Sherman began to bark, but like a good dog he didn't abandon me.

Okay, Jocelyn Graves! Get it together! You've got a job to do. Remember?

"Hey!" I yelled as I stepped out into the hallway. I didn't have my camera, but I had my phone. I fumbled with the screen and tapped the camera app. It opened, and I took a panoramic burst of photos. "Who is out here?" No one answered, and my voice echoed back to me. "Are you Moriah Mitchell? Mr. McCandlish? Ollie? Is that you?" Sherman barked once as a small shadow swept across the hall. And then all was still. I petted the dog on his head.

"Well, boy, if we're going to chase shadows, we better do it right. Come on," I said as I hurried back to my room to gather my audio recorder and anything else I could manage to carry. So much for research. The spirits of the Leaf Academy were stirring now, and I was ready to capture the evidence of their existence. *Non timebo mala.* I will fear no evil. I was beginning to understand why they had that engraved over the door. Had the builders of the Leaf Academy always known this place was a spiritual hot spot?

That's when I noticed the picture on my cot, but I'd just dropped it in the other room. I couldn't help but pick it up. Only there were figures missing from the sketch—the man in the leather jacket wasn't sitting beside me now. He was gone, and so was the boy.

I was sitting alone in the auditorium. With my neck twisted at an awkward angle.

What was this supposed to be? Some sort of freaky threat? This had to be a joke, an extremely jacked-up joke. But who would go to the trouble of pulling such a horrible gag on me? Pete Broadus wasn't this smart. And Midas? Never in a million years. Nobody knew where I was except Adrian Shanahan and Mr. Holloway.

Sherman began to growl at the doorway. "I know, I hear it too." I clicked on the digital recorder in hopes of recording the sounds of the footsteps. They weren't heavy ones but small ones, as if a petite lady or a child were pacing up and down the hallway.

"I can hear you out there. Why don't you come in? Don't be afraid. Is that you, Ollie?"

Sherman didn't move, and neither of us could look away as the doorknob began to slowly twist.

Chapter Twelve—Jocelyn

After a few seconds, my investigator's brain kicked in and I stepped back, reached for my camera and hit the video button. Whatever was on the other side of that door seemed to know what I intended. The twisting doorknob ceased, but that was just the calm before the storm.

Tap, tap, tap.

Loud, persistent tapping—no, make that banging—echoed from the wall next to me. I got the feeling that "it" wanted us out of the room. The first bang struck the wall on the left, that was the outer wall, and then it hit the one on the right. And then there was banging on the wall near the windows. I could hear the old windows shaking in the panes, and I prayed that they wouldn't break and shatter all over us. Poor Sherman began barking; he was clearly terrified, but I couldn't offer him any comfort. My dog never barked, never. I didn't blame him one bit. I was shaking in my hiking boots. The tapping became banging, horrible, life-threatening banging that offended not only my ears but also my nervous system. I never wanted to pee so bad in my life. I grabbed Sherman's collar to keep him from launching himself at the wall beside us when finally, unable to stand it anymore, I screamed, "Stop!"

To my surprise, it did. Sherman stopped barking too; he was panting now. I felt the same way, as if I couldn't quite catch my breath. I patted him on the head as I stared at the doorknob. It was all too quiet now.

And then the music started. Swelling orchestra music, like the kind you would hear if you were seated in the auditorium. I shivered as I thought about the horrible drawing with me sitting beside the ghost boy. Was that what this was about? Was the ghost boy trying to lead me to the auditorium? That's where they had found the very dead body of Hugh McCandlish in the fall of 1937. He'd been dead for many weeks, or at least that was what was printed in the newspaper at the time. For the life of me, I hadn't been able to locate a coroner's report or anything like it with Hugh McCandlish's name on it. Was this the Ollie spirit Mr. Mitchell referred to in his journal?

The music got louder. What was that tune? It seemed like I should know it from my college theater days. I walked to the window and with some elbow grease managed to open it a crack. I could hear people applauding, and now a woman was singing. Even though I could barely hear her, I knew this song!

Goodnight, my love, the tired old moon is descending
Goodnight, my love, my moment with you now is end-
ing
It was so heavenly, holding you close to me
It will be heavenly to hold you again in a dream

Immediately I began recording, but from this distance it wasn't going to be hi-def material. I had to get closer. I looked down at Sherman.

"Are you thinking what I'm thinking?" I asked him as I put the device back in my pocket and dug through his overnight bag for his leash. Snapping it on him, I patted his head and gave him a pep talk. He tugged back but didn't fight me too much as the music played on. *It could be an old record player I'm hearing.* The music did sound kind of scratchy, otherworldly.

The stars above have promised to meet us tomorrow
Till then, my love, how dreary the new day will seem
So for the present, dear, we'll have to part
Sleep tight, my love, goodnight, my love

"Okay, boy. This is for all the money. We've got to get close enough to record the sound; that means you can't run off and leave me. And be quiet, okay?" He whined and pushed his cold nose against my hand. "You can do this, Sherman Graves. You're a ghost hunter just like your Mom."

Together we faced the door, and I pressed my ear against it to make sure I couldn't hear anything in the hall. Obviously, there was a ton of activity in the building tonight, but the last thing I wanted to do was walk into Gary Holloway. *Hey, that's kind of trippy. Why is it dark in here?* It wasn't anywhere near sunset. Why did it feel like whatever intelligence was here—and I believed there *was* an intelligence operating here—wanted to keep this place in the dark?

Because you can't see what's hiding in the dark, and it doesn't want you to see it. Not yet.

As I put my hand on the doorknob, the music stopped. Even the sound of applause waned, but there was no turning back now. Clutching Sherman's leash tight, I swung the door open and immediately stepped out into the hallway.

"Hello?" I clicked on the recorder again. I had Sherman in one hand, the recorder in the other and a camera around my neck. I sure hoped I didn't have to take off running again. I wasn't graceful enough to navigate all three and my feet successfully.

I gasped at the sight of the boy standing near the upstairs landing. He had on dark clothing, but I could see quite a bit of detail like the dirty hems of his sleeves and pant legs. Yes, he was very dirty, as if he'd just dug his way out of his own grave. I couldn't see his hands or fingernails from here, but I was pretty sure that if I could I would see that they were filthy. His hair hung in his eyes, obscuring them from view, but I knew he was watching me.

Sherman growled; it was a low, menacing growl. My mouth went dry as I stared into the growing darkness at the face of the boy...or what pretended to be a boy. He didn't move except his head, which rolled slightly as if it weren't quite connected to his neck properly. Or was he reminding me of the picture?

"Ollie? Do you plan to kill me?" I asked without thinking. Why would I ask such a question?

He immediately turned away from me and headed to the top of the staircase without answering my question or offering any further acknowledgement. And there wasn't a sound in the place. No wind, no music, no skittering of rodents across the floor. I gripped the leash and the recorder and walked slowly toward the staircase.

This is why you're here, Jocelyn. Get the evidence. Stay focused. Don't hype yourself up.

Somewhere below me a door slammed, but that was the extent of the noise. Yes, it was quiet in here, too quiet. Sherman didn't make a sound except for his toenails on the grungy floor.

"Down the stairs now. We've got this, boy," I whispered as quietly as I could, an impossible task with the current echo level. With an unsure whimper, Sherman descended with me, and now I had mixed emotions. What was I doing bringing this poor dog here? The Leaf Academy was no place for a pet. Yep, I was a horrible parent. Maybe I should go. I was sure Adrian would understand if I explained the situation to her.

While I reasoned with my cowardly self, I caught a glimpse of something just below us. It was a pile of feathers, black feathers! They were in a triangular formation, deliberately placed where I could find them. As Sherman and I paused on the step, I could hear the song playing. That definitely had a record player feel to it.

Remember that you're mine, sweetheart
Goodnight, my love, your mommy is kneeling beside you
Goodnight, my love, to dreamland the sandman will guide you
Come now, you sleepyhead, close your eyes and go to bed
My precious sleepyhead, you mustn't play peek-a-boo

"I don't know what games you're playing, Ollie, but I'm not yours. And the only person who can call me Mommy is this dog. What do you want? Why are you hanging around here at the Leaf Academy?" I couldn't see him anymore, but I felt a presence—an angry, hateful presence—very near me.

Suddenly I was being shoved to the ground. A pair of small hands hit me in the lower back. Sherman scrambled away from me, and I lost my grip on his leash. I yelled for him as he ran toward the auditorium barking like a madman.

"Sherman!" I shouted as I got up as quickly as I could. I knew without looking that I'd broken my camera. I took it off my neck and set it on the ground while I dusted myself off. And he was there again.

The boy Hugh McCandlish called Ollie. He was a ghost boy, wasn't he? He smiled as if he heard my thoughts, as if he liked my wondering. He vanished as Sherman's desperate barking echoed through the bottom floor.

And then the furry white animal came yelping back to me. "Oh, thank God! What did I tell you, boy? Stay close to me! Are you okay?" I hugged him up as the door at the end of the hall slammed again. I rubbed the debris off my dog and waved at a persistent gnat that buzzed in my ear.

Glancing down both sides of the hall, I couldn't see much. Meager light filtered through a few slits in the boards but beyond that nothing. How in God's name was it this dark in here? I dug out my flashlight and waved it around. With each pass of the beam I saw shadows move, like they were living things eager to remain hidden.

Yeah, you know why, Jocelyn Graves. Non timebo mala.

I dug out my digital recorder. Sure, that Ollie-boy wanted me in that auditorium, but there was something here, an insistent presence I could not ignore. I wasn't running into that auditorium half-cocked. I was doing this investigation my way. If I let fear get the best of me, I would be giving all my power over to Ollie or that weirdo Gary Holloway. Strange that I would have such a thought. Was I sensing Gary near? I wasn't one to have sensitivities like that, not above the normal. And again that gnat buzzed in my ear. Or was that a mosquito? Either way, it was doing its level best to find a home in my ear. I swatted furiously as I kept Sherman close.

"Who is here with me? I know I am not alone. Tell me your name."

Sherman scratched himself as he panted; his full attention was on the end of the hall. All the sounds had stopped except for the horrible bug that was testing my fortitude. I swatted at it again and took a few steps toward the auditorium. Maybe I should go in there now. No sense in waiting until midnight. It was going to get lively tonight, I could tell. I stepped closer, but Sherman wasn't happy about that. I paused to listen.

No sound at all in there. Just the occasional flapping of wings.

Oh, God! What if it was full of crows? I hadn't seen any earlier, but that was before Ollie showed up. Collect the evidence, Jocelyn. Keep a level head.

I scanned back the audio on my digital recorder but didn't hear anything. May as well try again. "I know you're here. Can you tell me your name? Are you related to the boy, the one they call Ollie?" I waited a few seconds before turning it off.

The frantic buzzing stopped as I scanned the file back. I could hear myself, but there was someone else there too! Someone *was* communicating with me. I turned the volume up and scanned it back again. I didn't need audio software to pick that out.

Not a boy.

"Hugh? Hugh McCandlish? Is it you I am speaking to?" I squatted down to pet Sherman as I spun around on the balls of my feet to keep watch over my shoulder. I had the sensation that someone intended to get the drop on me, and I'd already been pushed down that last step. At least it wasn't the top step, but I didn't want to be surprised again. I scanned back the recording, but there was nothing else to hear. Nothing except Sherman's panting and my fear-filled voice.

A lighter clicked behind me, and I sprang to my feet. *Gary Holloway?* Cigarette smoke drifted in my direction, but Gary himself did not appear. I yelled as Sherman wrapped his leash around me. The cigarette smoke hovered in the air like a living thing, fluttered toward me and then dissipated into thin air.

"Gary Holloway? Is that you?"

But it wasn't Gary Holloway that manifested in the hallway. It was someone else, a tall man with a wild red beard and wide, terror-filled eyes. Before I could call out or say another word, he was walking toward me. And then through me! Cold like I'd never felt before covered me—no, it filled me. I felt a bit wobbly, kind of sick as I watched in horror as the tall, spindly man walked down the dark corridor. Although he never acknowledged me or spoke a word, I knew his name.

I was looking at the ghost of Hugh McCandlish!

And there was light coming from the auditorium.

And I was going in.

Chapter Thirteen—Hugh

My feet felt like two blocks of wood. They were so heavy that it took great force to lift them, but I continued on. It was as if my body did not want to go, but my heart would not allow me to turn back. Ollie was a prisoner of whatever darkness called the Leaf Academy home. It was an old darkness, to be sure, one I should have believed in, but it was too late now. Too late to go back and change the direction of my life, to change my plans. The faces around me had all but vanished, yet I heard a great ocean of whispering. With my hands covering my ears, I sobbed like a child as I stepped into the auditorium.

And there was Ollie, standing in the center of the stage, a helpless expression on his face. My feet felt free now, so I ran to the stage ignoring the slithering shadows around me. I hadn't forgotten that snakelike creature, the one with the scaly arms that had grabbed him so cruelly. "Ollie! Come here!"

And then I saw it—the creature! It was tall, taller than me. It was all black with scaly skin, like a dragon's skin, and its yellow eyes were focused on me. I saw Ollie's eyes widen as if he knew it was right behind him but he did not dare look. "Help me," I heard him whisper, but how could that be? His mouth didn't move. And his eyes...they were so dark. Ollie? Was this really Ollie LeFlore or something pretending to be him?

"McCandlish! Please, stop!"

"Headmaster? Thank God! Help me!" I thought I was speaking coherently, but my words came out as so much babbling. I turned back to reach for the boy, and he was gone. The black creature with the scaly skin crawled toward me; it was at the very edge of the stage. It could pounce on me at any moment. No! Those weren't just scales but also feathers! What in the name of God was this thing?

The headmaster raced toward me and gripped me by the shoulders. "What have you done? Have you accepted a gift from it? A feather, perhaps, or a stone? Tell me, Hugh."

I wanted very much to tell him that yes, I had found a feather and that he should help Ollie, but I couldn't make the words come out. Invisible hands were around my throat, choking me.

And then before my eyes the headmaster flew across the room and landed on the stage. The creature had vanished, but Ollie was there. And in his hands was a black feather. He walked to the headmaster, who was crying out in pain, and held it out to him. Clearly Ollie wanted him to take the feather, but the headmaster turned his back to him. His arm must have been broken for it was at a strange angle. The headmaster was crying—no, he was praying. It was in Latin. I knew that phrase. What was it? Oh yes, fear no evil. I will fear no evil. I closed my eyes and repeated the prayer.

But it was too late for me. I had accepted the feather. I had accepted his gift. I watched with great sadness as the headmaster slid off the stage and made his way out of the auditorium. He would not die, although he was badly hurt.

But me? I would certainly die. Unless I gave him what he wanted. He was leaning down over me now. His face changed from Ollie to the black creature. They were one and the same. I understood it now. The hands no longer choked me, but they held me down. What a horrible sight! And then it was the boy again with that familiar sad look on his face.

You promised. You said we would leave here. Take me. Let us go and you will live.

With all my might I wanted to live, to have a life and a family and a son. A good son. But I would have none of those things. I would never be the one to let this thing loose upon the world. Never.

I didn't have to say a word. It knew what I was thinking. With a rage-filled scream, it lighted on me and then I was no more.

Chapter Fourteen—Jocelyn

I pushed the door open easily enough. And unlike the first time I entered the room, it didn't make a sound. *That's weird*, I thought as I stepped inside the massive room. Sherman wasn't eager to join me, but I held the door open and he followed me inside. The auditorium wasn't any more appealing than it was before. There were rows of chairs upended, plaster from the ceiling and walls had fallen on the floor, and the holes in the exterior wall gave me a great view of the overgrown backyard. Yeah, this place was certainly atmospheric. I shook away thoughts of zombies crawling through the breaches.

Sherman barked and paced the aisle; his black nose was to the ground and waving back and forth as if he'd caught a whiff of something. "Sherman, stay close," I whispered as I squatted down to pet him. Immediately my eyes fell on the feather in front of me. This specimen was much shinier and larger than the other ones I'd found on the property. What kind of bird shed that thing? Not a crow. Couldn't be. Could a raven get that big? Maybe an owl? I'd never seen a black owl before. As I reached out to grab it, Sherman intercepted me, snapped up the feather and ran out of the auditorium. I was on my feet thinking to chase him when the door slammed between us. My dog began to bark frantically like he wanted me to know I was in trouble.

As if I didn't already know that. Yeah, I was in trouble. Big trouble. I turned out to face whoever it was that stood behind me.

I had heard no footsteps, yet I knew someone was there. Someone who didn't want me to leave. "Who's there?"

There was a boy, the one I'd captured on my camera earlier. "Ollie?" Fear crept into my bones as I asked the question. I wasn't one to run at the first sign of a spirit or a ghost, but this wasn't anything ordinary. Yeah, this wasn't your run-of-the-mill apparition. His dark eyes bored into mine. He hated me, that's what he wanted me to know. He hated me down to my bones. Why didn't I accept this present? He'd left it for me.

Where did that thought come from?

Sherman stopped barking, and I stepped back and away from the ghost. And as if there were truly a bird flying overhead, another feather floated down in front of me. It hovered in front of my face a few seconds before it fluttered to the ground. The boy stepped closer to me, his eyes not on me now but on the feather.

Take it. It's yours.

The boy's young voice filled my mind even though I did not see his mouth move. His hand was outstretched toward the feather. This was a gift from him, a gift of friendship. He wanted to be my friend, a special friend, but I had to accept his gift first. All his friends accepted gifts from him. I wouldn't be the first or the last, but I would be oh so special.

I couldn't think of anything I wanted less than to accept a gift from this entity. And then it dawned on me—this thing was offering me a gift because it wanted something in return. But what? This was beyond a residual imprint, and no way was this a run-of-the-mill intelligent haunt; I'd never met anything like this before. My investigator's mind raced through the catalog. What was I looking at? This ghost wanted me to enter a covenant with him.

Uh, no thanks. I took a step back. I shook my head no. The boy's face changed completely. Instead of a pale, doe-eyed boy with a shock of dark hair, I was looking at a horrible monster, a wraith with a skeletal face and a hand that reached for me.

Sherman barked furiously now, and I eased back, unsure of my footing. The floor felt weird, kind of spongy. I forgot all about my investigator's mindset and my digital recorder. I glanced down and could see that I was standing in a pile of feathers. *Oh, God! What is this?* I looked back up to see that Ollie wasn't alone now. There were others, including Gary

Holloway and a dead lady in a red dress. I was backing away faster now. I didn't dare turn my back on the growing crowd of spirits. Some I couldn't see, but I could certainly feel them. What the hell?

Hell is right, I heard a voice say mockingly inside my head. Was that Gary Holloway?

I reached for the door, but it wouldn't open. I had to turn around and take my eyes off the spirits. I had to put my full attention on getting it to move. "Come on! Come on!" I muttered, trying to stop myself from screaming my head off. I glanced over my shoulder as I banged on the door. Sherman barked up a storm, and I threw my shoulder into the effort to get the door open. Ollie was so close to me that I could almost hear him breathing. How was that possible? Ghosts didn't breathe. With a final bang and a savage kick with my boot, the door opened and Sherman shot through the open door to me.

"No, Sherman!" I yelled at him, praying that he wasn't going to get in a fight with this...whatever it was. "We have to go!" Piano music filled the auditorium, but there was no piano, only a rubble pile of keys and wood where a piano once stood. The music was loud, too loud to be just from a piano. The notes made no sense; it was merely angry noise, frightening, terrifying. I scooped up Sherman and leaped over another feather. *I can't touch it! I can't even touch it!*

Sherman barked continuously as I headed toward the front door.

"Oh, God!" I'd locked the door! The key! I reached around my neck and discovered it was gone. *No! Come on, give me a break!* What was I going to do now? There was nothing to do except face the music. I put Sherman down, and together we raced up the stairs. Maybe I took the necklace off up here? The horrible music still echoed from the auditorium, and now there were growls that accompanied it. Oh no! The boy stood at the top of the stairs.

I froze as Sherman whined beside me. The boy held out his hand and offered me a feather. "Take it. It's yours," he said with a sweet smile. I could hear him with my ears now.

"Too late, Ollie. I know what you really are," I said aloud.

"Do you?" he asked as the feather floated toward me.

I couldn't go up the stairs and get past him. I'd have to find another way out. Sherman was thinking ahead of me, apparently. I could hear his toenails clicking on the gritty floor below. I didn't hesitate either. I raced after him, praying that he could find a way out before this creature caught up with me. How many times could I refuse?

Sherman was running full speed down the corridor on the opposite side of the auditorium. There weren't any doors down here, were there? "Sherman!" I yelled, but the dog didn't wait for me.

Thanks a lot, boy.

I tripped once and landed face first on the ground but didn't break anything. My face felt dirty, and my eyes were having difficulty adjusting to the growing darkness. As I got up, I felt metal near my fingers. Oh, God! How did my key get down here? Yes! This was my leather necklace! I grabbed it as I hurried to my feet and tore down the corridor ignoring the feeling that things were following me, that they were piling out of the rooms ready to set upon me like wolves on a scared rabbit. *That's me, a scared rabbit!*

Sherman! You better wait for me, I thought with hot tears on my cheeks. I found him in a dirty room full of antique desks and chairs piled haphazardly atop one another. He hadn't been looking for a way out; he was looking for a place to hide!

"Come on, boy. It's okay. It's me." He whimpered and cowered under a desk. Why would he do that? I glanced over my shoulder as a shadow passed the doorway. Cautiously, I turned my head slightly, not absolutely sure that I wanted to see.

Please don't let this be Ollie.

It wasn't. I caught a quick glimpse of an unhappy face and knew it belonged to Hugh McCandlish! It must have been Hugh who had left the key where I could find it. But then he was gone. "We have to go, Sherman. We can't stay here another minute." I picked him up, and thankfully he didn't fight me.

With my dog in my arms, I ran back down the hall. I was terrified, of course, but I was also angry. Angry at myself that I had brought my dog to a horrible place like this. Angry that I hadn't listened to Midas but instead had come to the Leaf Academy like a high schooler hell-bent on mischief. I had put us both in a bad situation.

"It's okay, Sherman. It's going to be okay," I promised, hoping that I could make that be the truth. There was no sign of Ollie, no sign of the lady in red. Even the music had stopped. Whatever power Hugh had, he was using it. He must be, or else I wouldn't be leaving so freely. Sherman struggled now, but I refused to put him down. I warned him to stay still as I opened the front door and we scrambled out of the house.

It was raining now. I hadn't heard it raining inside, but it was coming down in buckets. Yet the sun was shining! What in the world? It hadn't been raining when I was in the auditorium. I would have seen it; I would have seen rain pouring through the holes in the walls and roof. This was no ordinary rainstorm.

*Forget about it, Jocelyn Graves. Just forget about it.
You can ponder the meaning of it all later.*

I raced to the car, but not before plunging into a
mudhole twice. I shoved the key in the ignition and
raced down the driveway. I wasn't looking back. Not
any time soon.

Chapter Fifteen—Jocelyn

"Hey, Jocelyn. I'm so happy to finally meet you in person. I'm Adrian. You'll have to pardon Mr. Holloway's absence. I'm afraid he's taken a turn for the worse."

"I had no idea he was sick. I am sorry to hear that. And thanks for sending your maintenance guy to help me retrieve all my things. I feel a bit like a chicken, but once I tell you everything, I think you'll understand." Adrian nodded politely. She had a round face, perfect makeup and lovely dark hair that she kept swept back from her face with a barrette. She was dressed professionally, whereas I looked like I just rolled out of bed in my torn jeans and bleached Ireland t-shirt. "And I really am sorry to hear about Mr. Holloway."

"He is such a nice man. Really active until he turned eighty; then it was just downhill from there. I know he hates that. He's always been such a force of nature, at least in our family."

"Oh," I said with surprise in my voice. I unzipped my laptop bag and pulled out my computer carefully. "I didn't know you two were related."

"He's my grandfather."

"I'm sorry I didn't put that together. Does that mean you'll be handling the Leaf Academy property someday? I know you said you didn't enjoy going there."

"Yes, I think so. My children and I are the only Holloways left, and I most certainly don't want to pass the property down to them if it's as bad as I suspect."

I turned on the laptop but paused before digging out the jump drive. This lady was very afraid of the spirits of the Leaf Academy. She had reason to be, I could not lie about that, but I couldn't leave her feeling helpless. I decided I would do my best to give her some hope and offer her something she could use to battle the forces that believed the deserted building was their home.

"I wish I could tell you how to put an end to the goings-on there. I really do. Unfortunately, that's not in my wheelhouse; however, I know someone who may be able to help you. His name is Midas Demopolis. He's a friend of mine and the leader of Gulf Coast Paranormal. I saw a lot at the Leaf Academy, but it will take a team to really dig into the place's activities. I'm going to consult with him, if you don't mind. I don't want to dump this information on you and leave you to deal with it on your own."

"Really? You would do that?" She dabbed at her eyes with a tissue. I sure didn't mean to make her cry.

"Of course I will. I think you should know that bringing peace to that property is going to be a process. It is not going to be a one-smudge-and-done job. You'll have to call on whatever faith you have if you want to rid the place of the current residents."

"So it is haunted? For sure? No doubt in your mind? My grandfather always believed that. He believed that the Leaf Academy killed his brother. Is that possible?"

"The Leaf Academy is haunted and in a deeply malevolent way. There's something old there, maybe even ancient." She was taken aback by my comment. *Rein it in, Jocelyn. Show the evidence.* "I found this journal while I was exploring the place. I'm surprised no one else spotted it." I dug the dusty book, along with the drawings I'd tucked in it, out of my backpack and slid it toward her.

She flipped it open as she slid on her glasses. "What's all this?"

"I found this journal in one of the rooms on the second floor. It belonged to Moriah Mitchell, the headmaster of the Leaf Academy when Hugh McCandlish was murdered."

"Really? I hired someone to remove all those boxes, all the personal stuff. Apparently they didn't get everything." She began skimming through the pages. "What's this?" she asked as she removed one of the drawings. The expression on her face said it all. She thought it was disgusting too. "Wait...is this you?" She looked at me closely and then at the drawing.

"Yes, I think so. So much happened; I hardly know where to start, Adrian."

"Did you draw these? Because they look really old."

"I think they are really old. Probably at least eighty years old. If I had to guess, I would say that the boy, the one that Hugh McCandlish called Ollie and the same one that Mitchell refers to in his journal, was the artist. Here's where it gets weird; I don't believe he's actually a boy at all. He may never have been a boy."

"Really? Why do you say that?"

"Well, I have a theory, but I'd like to show you the rest of the evidence I have for you first."

She let out a deep breath and said, "Okay, I'm ready."

"This was the first day. I caught the image of the boy like right off the bat." I plugged my jump drive into the laptop and pulled up the folder of images I planned to show her. There he was, the 'boy' Ollie. "You can see the hair, the profile of his face. This is his arm." I pointed at the screen.

"Oh my God. I can see him!" Her hands flew to her mouth. "My grandfather was telling the truth all along. He saw him too, when he was a teenager, before his brother died. And here in this photo, this...spirit looks so lifelike. And you saw this with your own two eyes?"

"Wait. Mr. Holloway saw him?"

"Yes, but he doesn't like to talk about the encounter much. His father owned the place before him, and he and his brother spent many summers there trying to repair it. Old Mr. Holloway wanted to make the place an office complex, but it never worked out. After Gary died, my great-grandfather was so devastated that he never wanted to do anything else there. All the work stopped."

"I can understand that." I showed the shaken brunette a few more pictures and then clicked on the audio file. "Listen to this, Adrian."

I played the friendly "come find me" first and then the growls I'd captured in the auditorium. Suddenly, Adrian began to wipe at her eyes. She was clearly horrified.

"And this horrible thing is connected to my family. It killed my great-uncle. God forbid my grandfather passes and I have to handle this. I want to sell the place, but how can I? Who's going to buy it? I never liked going in there, and now I know why."

I had more to show her; I hadn't even reviewed the hours and hours of audio and video. But this was enough. I closed the laptop. "Are you okay? Can I get you a glass of water?"

She smiled politely and dried her eyes one more time. "Yes, I will be fine. It's just I half-hoped it was just a story, just a family legend, but it can't be. And how did you get those pictures? I don't understand. Something in that journal has you disturbed too."

In for a penny, in for a pound.

"There are several different kinds of hauntings, residual, intelligent..."

"I've seen some of the ghost hunting shows. I think I understand that part, Jocelyn. Clearly, this thing is intelligent. Right?"

"Yes, but it's more than that. I think what's at the Leaf Academy is extremely rare. There are ghosts, many of them, as you may have already guessed. But I don't think they want to be there. I think that the negative entity—this thing that pretends to be a little boy named Ollie—is actually what's known as a maelstrom. Have you ever heard of that?"

She shook her head, her eyes locked on me. "No, what is it?"

"Like I said, it's a rarity. Maelstroms create pandemonium wherever they appear. From what we know—the paranormal community, I mean—these maelstroms draw unhappy spirits to them and capture them, like a spiritual whirlwind. They don't willingly let the trapped spirits go, nor do they move on once they've established themselves in a location. Not easily. Maelstroms gain strength from the captured spirits, and it is this entity's goal to continue to add to its unhappy community."

"How did it get there? Is it human?"

"I don't believe it is human, but it might have been a very long time ago. How it got there? I can't tell you that either, but it has been lurking there for ages, at least as long as the academy was open. Moriah Mitchell knew about 'Ollie,' and he had to have heard about him from someone. He tried to help Hugh McCandlish, but he wasn't strong enough or prepared enough to take it on. Maelstroms like to play mind games with their targets. Like this picture. It was playing with me, threatening to kill me. Luckily for me, my dog was with me. He saved my life."

"Really?"

"Yeah." I shuddered at the thought. "I am really sorry about prematurely ending the investigation, but the truth is I wasn't prepared for it either. It is strong, and it wants out of there. Right now it can't get out, but who's to say it won't try again?"

"What are my options? Burn it to the ground?" Adrian eyed me seriously.

"Would that help? I couldn't say, but I promise you this isn't over. Gulf Coast Paranormal, that's Midas' team, they can help you and they won't charge you a thing. Please, let me call him before you do anything. It's worth a shot, right?"

"Yes, it is. If it brings peace to my family or to the spirits trapped there, I am willing to wait. I just hope we can figure it all out before my grandfather leaves this world."

I squeezed her hand. "We'll try, Adrian."

"And you'll call this Midas person for me?"

"I'll do it tonight."

Half an hour later, I left Adrian's realty office and headed home. No, it wasn't mission accomplished, but Sherman and I had made it out alive. And that was all that mattered. My heart went out to Adrian. It really did. I hoped that Midas could and would help her.

We'd have to see about that. In the meantime, I had to go home.

My best friend was waiting for me.

Epilogue—Jocelyn

A good hot shower for me and a nice soapy bath for Sherman helped set my mind at ease, but there was one last thing to do. Did I really want to do it? Gosh, why was this so hard? I was pretty sure he wasn't going to say no.

Screw it. I'm doing it.

I tapped the number on the screen and waited for him to pick up. I cleared my throat awkwardly as I heard his voice on the phone. "Hey, Aaron? It's me, Jocelyn. I was wondering if you liked pizza. I mean, did you have plans for dinner? Because I was thinking about grabbing a slice or two. I thought it might be nice to have someone to talk with, besides my dog."

His warm laugh filled my ears, and I instantly felt better. "No plans, and pizza sounds perfect. Nothing exotic, though. No pineapple for me."

"No pineapple for me either. I'm a pepperoni girl. See you at the Golden Mushroom? Around six?"

We agreed on the details and I hung up the phone. I was so glad Aaron didn't say anything skeezy or flirty. Pete used to do that all the time, and it drove me crazy. I didn't like my relationships filled with a lot of innuendo or flirtatious banter. Okay, once in a while, but not every conversation.

So, I was doing this, right?

I had one more call to make. The phone rang a few times, and just when I was ready to hang up I heard Midas' voice on the line. "Hey, Jocelyn. Glad to hear from you. Are you back home?"

"Yeah, I got home yesterday."

"I take it you found what you were looking for?"

"And more. Listen, I'm calling to let you know that I wear a medium and I will need at least two shirts. I don't do laundry as faithfully as I should."

"I've got those. Does this mean you'll be going to Gulfport with us?"

"I'd like to, if there's room still. I don't want to bump anyone if the van is full."

"Not full, and we're taking the SUV too. There's plenty of room."

I tossed Sherman his yellow squeaky ball, which he immediately brought back. "I went to the Leaf Academy, Midas. I hate to admit this, but I'm totally out of my league. Gathering evidence? No problem. Telling the client she has a maelstrom on her property? The pits."

The line went so quiet I could have heard a pin drop. At least he didn't say I told you so. "You're okay, though?"

"Yes, thanks to my dog and a ghost named Hugh McCandlish. I was hoping you could talk to Adrian, maybe connect her with a local ministry that has experience with evicting maelstroms. Someone that would be committed for the long haul 'cause it's not going to be an easy task."

"Of course I will. You'll have to fill me in."

I breathed a sigh of relief. "Thanks, Midas. I appreciate that." I smiled and threw Sherman his toy again. "One more thing...I called Aaron, and we're going to have pizza tonight. I just thought you should know."

"Great. I'm sitting here with Cassidy. We're headed to the Causeway for seafood and beers. And for the record, I don't have to know all the details of your personal life. I know you, Jocelyn. You always behave like a professional."

Images of me running from the Leaf Academy with my dog in my arms and falling in the mud not once but twice filled my mind. Nobody had to know about that, did they? Everyone loses their nerve once in a while. *Right, big professional here.* I glanced at the load of camera equipment still piled up by the front door. I was in no hurry to review the remainder of the evidence, but I would—in the next day or seven. I'd been very selective about what I'd shown Adrian, and I had a sneaking suspicion there was so much more.

"Thanks for the vote of confidence. Y'all have a good night."

"You too, Jocelyn." He hung up the phone, and I wrestled with Sherman for a while. He was so happy to be home with me, he didn't even try to follow me when I walked to the door in my little black dress and dress sandals a few hours later.

"I'll be back, Sherm. Don't wait up."

As I closed the door and locked it behind me, I heard the flicking of a lighter. The old-fashioned kind. I froze momentarily but didn't look back. No, I wouldn't look back. I just wasn't that kind of person. I didn't run exactly, but I hurried to the car and headed to the pizza joint.

Time to leave the dead behind. At least for a little while.

Read more from M.L. Bullock

The Nike Chronicles

Blue Water
Blue Wake
Blue Tide

The Seven Sisters Series

Seven Sisters
Moonlight Falls on Seven Sisters
Shadows Stir at Seven Sisters
The Stars that Fell
The Stars We Walked Upon
The Sun Rises Over Seven Sisters
Ghost on a Swing (series prequel)

The Idlewood Series

The Ghosts of Idlewood
Dreams of Idlewood
The Whispering Saint
The Haunted Child

Return to Seven Sisters
(A Seven Sisters Sequel Series)

The Roses of Mobile
All the Summer Roses
Blooms Torn Asunder
A Garden of Thorns

To receive updates on her latest releases,
visit her website at MLBullock.com
and subscribe to her mailing list.

About the Author

Author of the best-selling *Seven Sisters* series and the *Desert Queen* series, M.L. Bullock has been storytelling since she was a child. A student of archaeology, she loves weaving stories that feature her favorite historical characters—including Nefertiti. She currently lives on the Gulf Coast with her family but travels frequently to explore the southern states she loves so much.

Made in the USA
Columbia, SC
12 October 2021